B U K O W S K I
the
UBERMENSCH

Wayne F. Burke

INTRODUCTION

IT would be a thankless task to try and separate the reality of the flesh & blood and protoplasmic being known as Charles Bukowski from his auto-mythography—recorded in nearly fifty volumes of poetry and prose. It is not my intent, in any case, to try and do so; nor is it my intent to write a biography. My intent is to bring to light as much of the life as is necessary to the writing of a critique and analysis as well as review of the work.

In consideration of "autobiographical fiction" (an oxymoron, I realize) which was Bukowski's métier, exposition of some of the life is helpful, even necessary to a textual elucidation.

I will elucidate out front: to me, Bukowski, as human being, often approaches likeness of a stinking bag of human shit. I am not, however, dwelling here on the personal but on a critical approach, primarily, to the work.

I separate the above judgement whenever I read the work—which I have the highest regard for. In any case, I have come to criticize Bukowski not to bury him. Others have buried him before my arrival on scene: I speak of the politically correct, the ultra-feminists (whomever they be) and the poetry cognoscenti ("it is not poetry, it is chopped prose"—Hayden Carruth).

Reading Bukowski's work gave me the idea, as a writer as well, that my life, though not particularly exciting, or even interesting, to me, could be used as subject. That the writing about a life, no matter the circumstances of that life—how boring or uninteresting it is perceived to be—could, via writing, be made exciting and interesting to others. In his work Bukowski infused the quotidian of his existence with drama and hence, excitement. Through the magic of language he made the ordinary, the mundane, into something special…What I had as a young man, to work with, Buk helped me realize, was the life I was born to. Being a "somebody" or having extravagant experiences was not a pre-requisite for good, or even bad, writing. The writing gives value to the life, rather than vice-versa (not to deny the power of life reciprocally feeding the writing—something "Buk" insisted upon).

The first of Bukowski's books I read was titled BURNING IN WATER DROWNING IN FLAME, his 1974 Selected Poems. Read as I sat in a tiny shack along a road outside a big Ford Motor Company plant on the outskirts of Framingham, Massachusetts. I sat there be-cause my job, as security guard, required it.

I had scored the job from a guy who had picked me up while I was hitch hiking. I agreed to hire on because I'd always wanted a job at which I could read, as well as get paid. From 11 p.m. to 7 a.m. I sat in my shack, my feet usually up on a shelf, and me leaning back in a swivel chair—the shack windowed on all sides and heated by a vent below the chair.

Reading—until a truck pulled-up beside the shack. Then I would have to get up, go outside, and lift a twenty foot long aluminum pole, allowing the truck access to the yard.

I loved the poems of that book. I could not only understand them but could relate as well. Hell, the guy was describing aspects of my life and my feelings; putting into language some of my thoughts on the state of the world, and of existence. The poet had attitude also: an attitude I admired. A guy poet, who, simply put: did not seem to give a shit about much of anything; who did not stand on formalities or ceremony; who did not respect bourgeois notions of propriety. He seemed—the "I" of the verse seemed—to me, like a sort of freaking hero. Also something of a lady's man (though the lady's often labeled "whore") judging from the number of women who sashayed through the poetry.

God, how I wanted to also be a lady's man! How I too longed to give no shits'! Caring was painful (like work). To be a kind of "frozen man"—a term Bukowski used to describe his younger self (that is, emotionally frozen, withdrawn) seemed, to me, a better way to be: a more efficacious way to immure myself from unpleasant and brutal realities…Or would it? Hell, what did I know? I was nineteen years old and, recently, a college drop-out. My 3rd time, in two years, dropping out of college; and other than an idea of becoming some kind of writer (journalist maybe?) I had no clue as to what to do with myself. None, baby!

I often slept on the job.

One night, sound asleep, I awoke to the vibration of the earth and shack. I thought it was an earthquake, until I came-to, realized where I was, and noticed the truck outside my door; a big sucker: a ten-wheeler loaded with automobiles. I stumbled out into the night, under a deep sea blue sky of stars like a diamond-studded field…I pulled down on a 3-foot long handle to elevate the long pole: The truck moved ahead. The stars twinkled. I dropped the pole. It landed on top the truck's cab and bent into the shape of a horseshoe…The truck horn sounded like the moan of a stricken beast. The driver barked at me like a chained and hungry dog. I heard other voices as well; the lights of the yard came on blazing, illuminating the crime scene.

Good Christ!

Some guy of dark mien screamed in my face…Who was he and where did HE come from?

Wtf? Everyone makes a mistake now and then, right?

The screams finally chilled and the night turned quiet again, except for the low roar of the plant, which was constant. The truck had moved ahead…For all subsequent trucks arriving that night I had to elevate the pole only a foot or so to allow access.

The next Buk title read was FACTOTUM, his 1975 novel. Not having enough money to buy the book, I visited the bookstore daily and read from the book each visit, standing or kneeling in the aisle as I read. People said "excuse me" as they moved past but I never let them distract me: I read on, and on, but drawing so many unfriendly looks from the bookstore staff I decided to cease and pick it back up at a later date.

I did pay for a copy of Bukowski's ERECTIONS, EJACULATIONS, EXHIBITIONS, and General Tales of Ordinary Madness (City Lights, 1972), bought at the Harvard Coop Bookstore in Cambridge, Massachusetts, where Harvard University lives. I lived, at the time, in the Central Square YMCA, and worked as fry cook in a restaurant in Harvard Square. I kept the job until the night I got beat-up in a Central Square bar and showed up to work in the morning wearing mirror sunglasses, to cover my blackened eyes. The Indian owner—he called me "Vane," fired me. Oh well. I subsequently went to work part-time as janitor for Harvard University. I stole books out of the professor's offices I cleaned and sold the books to the Coop. That is how I got the money to buy the Bukowski title.

Always on the look-out for other Bukowski titles: I read a few stories he'd published in HIGH TIMES magazine, the magazine for the stoner-set, and which my college roommate (I was back in school—not Harvard), a dedicated druggie, subscribed to. No Bukowski titles were assigned in any of the college English courses I took. His work was 'outside' reading for me—reading that got me onto academic probation. Ignoring assigned texts in favor of books of my choice led to my downfall as college-boy at the first three, of four, institutions of higher learning I attended (the 4th, GODDARD COLLEGE, allowed students to devise their own curriculum, and to grade themselves as well. I graduated from the place summa cum laude and with a BA Degree in Liberal Arts—1979).

Enough about me. This is not a book about me but about Bukowski, the "Ubermensch," a German term that roughly translates to English as

"Superman." The Yiddish "mensh" is defined as a man of rectitude and dignity who has a sense of what is right, and is responsible and decorous. To be called a "real mensh" is an ultimate compliment. German definition of "mensch" is also a man, person, individual, but without special connotation bestowed by the Yiddish. German definition of "uber," small 'u', is "over; above, on top of…" So: we have a Bukowski, a man on top of, above, over; maybe not a "real" mensh but definitely an "Ubermensch."

Contents

JUST THE FACTS, MAM

Heinrich Karl Bukowski was born in Andernach, Germany, August 16, 1920. His father, at the time, was an American G.I. stationed in Germany, and was himself of German ancestry; his parents having immigrated to America from Germany. Bukowski's mother was a German citizen, named Katherine, maiden name "Fett." She worked as a seamstress (pg. 7, Howard Sounes, CHARLES BUKOWSKI, Locked in the Arms of a Crazy Life). The family relocated in 1923, Germany to Baltimore, U.S.A, and then to Pasadena, California, which was the father's, Henry Senior's, hometown.

The paternal grandparents were estranged from one another. The grandfather, Leonard, was in the construction business (pg. 10, Barry Miles, CHARLES BUKOWSKI) and owned several houses. He was not an active part of young Henry's life. He was, reportedly, alcoholic. Two of Bukowski's Uncles, John and Ben, Henry Senior's brothers, were also reportedly alcoholic. Henry Senior, the father, hated drunks (geez, I wonder why). The grandmother was something of a religious crank or fanatic. "A strict Baptist" (pg. 8 Sounes). In Bukowski's poem "death of an idiot" an odd boy of the neighborhood—he spoke to mice and birds, dies at age 16. The young unnamed boy appears to be Bukowski himself who dies, metaphorically, spiritually, as idiot child. Dies to the father who daily beat and abused the boy—in the poem. The grandmother of the poem arrives to pray for the child, asking the devil to let loose his hold on the idiot boy. When Hank (Charles) was fifteen and broken-out in boils due to acne vulgaris the grandmother came to the house to pray for him, brandishing a crucifix and yelling "purge the devil from his body Lord" (pg. 32 Miles). The woman was of gross appetite according to her grandson and not very interesting as a person (but "few are" Bukowski wrote).

The Bukowski's started their life as Angeleno's in a house in a poor neighborhood south of downtown. Hank (Henry Jr.) was not allowed by his parents to play with the neighborhood children. His parents thought themselves superior to their neighbors. Hank was not dressed like the American children but in more formal wear, like the clothes of European children—in velvet trousers and shirts with frilly collars (pg. 9 Sounes). An anomaly in the neighborhood, young Hank stuck-out from the crowd like an albino buffalo from a herd, and was picked-on with taunts of "Heine" due to his German heritage.

Henry Senior worked as a delivery man for a creamery, driving a cart pulled by a horse. The same job as David Schearl's father, Albert, held—in Henry Roth's famous novel CALL IT SLEEP (1934). (The fictional Albert rivals the real Henry Senior in brutality and crudeness toward their respective sons.) Henry Senior began beating Hank around the time Hank entered Grammar School. Whipping the boy with a razor strop. The "psychopathic" father, Bukowski biographer Barry Miles writes, who beat the boy while the "stupid, cowed" mother watched (pg. 26 Miles).

The family moved twice during Hank's formative years. The house Hank grew-up in—so-called "house of horrors" to Bukowski—was on South Longwood Avenue. Hank did not do well in school, possibly because of dyslexia; also because of his being an "other" to classmates due to Hank's oddity—his German heritage— and his parent's strictures not allowing him to mingle with the other children. Not until ingratiating himself with the others did Hank cease being "Heine" and became "Hank."

At Mount Vernon Junior High School Hank won praise for his writing from an English teacher who read aloud an essay he had written ("Mrs. Fretag" in Buk's novel HAM ON RYE).

When Hank was around thirteen years old he was pulled out of school to undergo treatment for his acne vulgaris, at L.A. County Hospital.

At home and alone one day, and between trips to the hospital, Hank filled a notebook with a story written about World War I flying ace Baron von Richthofen who, despite an iron hand (one hand had been shot off), downed plane after enemy plane. Metaphor as wish fulfillment: von Richthofen, maimed, like Hank by his acne, triumphs in heroic fashion despite his affliction.

It must have been a hard life for young Hank who, though an only child and thus privileged to receive all the attention of his parents, was beaten regularly (or, as his father probably put it: "disciplined.") Less attention would probably have benefited Hank far more.

As youngster Hank looked to his mother for protection against the father. Looked at her "impartial and tasteless iron face" (pg. 140, Bukowski, NOTES OF A DIRTY OLD MAN). The mother failed him miserably, being unable to stand-up to her husband. Or refusing to. Remaining instead the obedient and submissive wife.

The mother's failure to protect is at the root of Bukowski's less than flattering opinion of women in general. The childhood scenario discolored Hank's attitude toward women. Young Hank had to have questioned his mother's love for him, for after all, if the mother did love him, why would she not protect him? Or even side with him against the father? The mother, by extension, became all-women, or WOMAN. Stupid and cowed, undeserving of his, the abused child's, respect. The child, such as Hank, unable to understand the mother's fear, a fear bred through her indoctrination via an upbringing in strict parameters of a traditionally patriarchal society—that affected her choices…The child only knows the pain of the abuse and feels consequently helpless in the situation—and that the mother is no help—because she does not WANT to help: she allows the abuse to continue through her nonintervention, and thus, allowing the abuse, becomes, by extension, an ally of the father-abuser, not of the child.

The mother is seen, by the child, as weak, possibly even evil or as hateful as the father. Also, any sympathy she, Hank's mother, extended to him was the sympathy of another victim, for she too was being beaten.

In youthful years Hank spent much time in the local library reading an eclectic line-up of authors. He came to admire D. H. Lawrence's style (is there any writer who does not?). He was also impressed by three other writers, each very different as stylists: Ernest Hemingway, John Fante, and William Saroyan. Hemingway for the clarity of language and style; Fante for the raw emotionalism of his protagonists; and Saroyan for an instantly recognizable narrative voice.

WILLIAM SAROYAN

Bukowski claimed that Saroyan's early work influenced his own writing.

Saroyan's story is like a parable from out the American Success God's notebook.

Saroyan published a book of short stories in 1933, one of the worst years of the Great Depression. The narrative voice of THE DARING YOUNG MAN ON THE FLYING TRAPEZE instantly won readers: insouciant, playful, and joyous in spite of the ongoing national tragedy and pain; a voice of irrepressible joie de vivre—just what the country wanted to hear. The collection sold over 6,000 copies, an unheard of number for a short story collection. Saroyan rocketed to literary heights.

William, or Bill, had been born in Fresno, California, in 1908, to Armenian parents, first generation immigrants who had settled on the West coast of America and survived by working at unskilled laboring jobs (only work they could get). The father died, age 36, after he ruptured his appendix. The mother, alone, could not cope and put her four children into an orphanage. Where they lived for a handful of years before reunited through the mother's efforts. William was age 8 at the time of reunion; he peddled newspapers and delivered telegrams to make a buck. In school, he proved himself difficult, over-sensitive to criticism and disdainful of authority. In time, he became a difficult adult, with an arrogant sense of entitlement exemplified by an imperious manner.

When subsequent publications of his stories failed to equal the commercial success of his first book, Saroyan turned to the theater and wrote two plays—"My Heart is in the Highlands," and "The Time of Your Life," that made him, for a short period, the hottest playwright on Broadway.

After his marriage to a debutante (actress Carol Marcus: she 18, he 34) Bill was drafted into the U. S. Army and became an unhappy private and a disgruntled human being.

The popularity of Saroyan's subsequent writings fell as quickly as his meteoric rise. Unwilling to take criticism of any sort—relying on his native "genius," he failed to grow as an artist, and continued using the same old tropisms that had wrought his early success. In a way, he became a casualty of the war years, in that the naivety and innocence reflected through the voice of his stories sounded ever more distant and unbelievable in the face of new realities of a cynical and hardened post-war Age of the Bomb. He, and his work, became something of a repetitious bore. He became, one critic wrote, "a middle-aged man on a sighing trapeze" (pg. 285, John Legget, A DARING YOUNG MAN, A Biography of William Saroyan). Saroyan's brave optimism buoyed people up in the depression years, but "turned to sugar water/during/good times," wrote Bukowski in his poem "the still trapeze."

Like Buk, Saroyan was prolific, publishing over fifty books in his lifetime. Both were depression-era writers whose works carry the era's knowledge of want and need. Buk, I believe, the far greater writer, but perhaps a lesser artist ("artist"? What is that? Buk: "an artist…says a difficult thing in a simple way"—pg. 166, NOTES). Bukowski's voice is easily recognizable and relatable as well: wry and tougher, more cynical, than Saroyan's; likewise, as congenial, but without the whining sentimentality, verging on bathos, that Saroyan more than occasionally indulged in. Unlike Buk, Saroyan was not alcoholic yet was an addict all the same: addicted to the highs and lows of gambling. Like Buk in his alcoholically-induced "misadventures," Saroyan also, again and again, devastated his existence, through one gambling debacle after another, at race track, ballfield, and at the poker and baccarat tables. He knew better, but could not stop himself. Gambling, travel, and spending money gave him something he could not get elsewhere. I assume the excitement took him, momentarily, out of his self; a place he did not want to be. Where the insecurities of the orphanage and poverty of his youth resided.

Both writers were egotistical monsters of a particular kind (like Hemingway, Joyce, Celine, Hamsun, Dahlberg, and Fante) who felt that because of their "genius" they could do and act as they pleased, and mostly without recourse for feelings trampled upon and corpses left in their wake.

Saroyan particularly suffered because of his raging Tribalism. His tribe those Armenians, relatives and friends, whom he both loved and loathed. The outside world—those outside the pale—Saroyan distrusted, viewing them, at large, as enemies trying to deprive him a place in the sun.

In his last years—after a short revival of interest in his short stories, Saroyan became, in the decade of the 1970's, something of a Timon of Fresno, sitting on his fortune and warring against a small army of lawyers, publishers, executors, doctors, retailers, and IRS agents. A sad end, in retrospect. Saroyan could not extract the beam from his own eye. Accurate self-analysis eluded him (or he discounted such as applicable). He became a cantankerous prematurely aged old man, estranged from family and recognized not so much as a great artist as possessor of a great white walrus-moustache…A monarch of a world without truly fit subjects besides himself.

He died from prostate cancer, age 73, the same age Charles Henry Bukowski died—a monarch also.

"BUK" AS IN "PUKE"

By the age of sixteen Hank had discovered the efficacy of alcohol. The booze made him feel bigger, stronger, and, somehow, smarter. Which for someone like Hank, battling an inferiority complex, was a tremendous gift. Through use of booze he is, or can be, a participant in life instead of perpetual outsider and observer. Momentarily, he found courage— courage enough to cold-cock his father, who, by Hank's recollection, quit the fight (just like a "bully"—an essentially gutless specimen).

Of course, the booze lies as it seduces. Tells wondrous fibs. The great deceiver alcohol promises greatness and grandeur but leaves the drinker sick and emptied. Gives the drinker wings to fly then takes away the sky. But that taking occurs down the road in an alcoholic's alcoholic life. When the booze is still working—producing the euphoria that becomes, in itself, so addictive to the drinker (budding alcoholic), it is wonderful; but when it stops working, producing other lesser feelings than euphoria, or else deadening all feeling (leaving one in the "Frozen Man" condition) the booze, like a thief, is steals time, money, and eventually life.

In High School, 1936, Bukowski had a fling with Fascism. A fling he felt, later, embarrassed about. He and his mother declared Nazi sympathies (like a majority of Germans in Germany—or 37.9% at least) and became members of the German-American Bund. Hank wrote letters to the editor supportive of Hitler which were published in the Los Angeles Examiner newspaper (pg. 38 Miles). In a charitable interpretation, Hank was trying to reconnect to his German heritage, which he had been separated from since the age of three. Less charitably, and maybe more accurately, he and mother, feeling small and weak, sought antidote to those feelings through identification with fascist ideology and the greater party—exemplified by National

Socialism. Hank has written that his major impetus for support of Hitlerism was his reaction against the true-blue Americanism of classmates, teachers, and neighbors (and his father, who wrapped himself in the American flag). A case of Hank's streak of contrariness—as well as case of caging drinks off the "right-wingers," Hank later wrote. Reacting, through his feelings of alienation, against a status quo represented by those "normal" others, such as the achievers and accomplished "winners" of his more well-to-do L.A. High School classmates. (Hank had attended Susan Miller Dorsey High School for a year, prior to enrolling at L.A. High—pg. 18, David Stephen Catonne, CHARLES BUKOWSKI, Critical Lives.)

Hank also joined R.O.T.C. (Reserve Officer's Training Corps) in High School. Given choice of gym or R.O.T.C., he chose the latter, not because of interest in the military, but because, in gym class, he would have had to take off his clothes and thus reveal the state of his skin condition—something he was loath to do.

Hank went dateless through High School. He thought himself unattractive, not loveable; girls were solely creatures of his fantasies.

After High School graduation, in 1939, Hank began work as a stock-boy for Sears & Roebuck Company (pg. 45, Neeli Cherkovski, BUKOWSKI, A Life) a job he was fired from after getting into a fight, inside the store, with a former High School classmate (pg. 18 Sounes).

After the stint as stock-boy Hank returned to school, enrolling in Los Angeles City College. As a scholarship student studying journalism.

An English professor at the college praised Hank's writing—the 2nd of his school teachers to do so.

Hank took only courses he wanted to take as he continued his autodidactic education, spending much time in the college library, and in the L. A. Public Library.

Hank left college in '41 after 2 years of sporadic attendance. He earned no journalism certificate but became, in a way, a sort of journalist, reporting on news of himself. Giving readers, in his many books of poetry, the low-down, skinny, real dope on his activities. Sometimes the reports manufactured, as in exaggerated, embellished, even fabricated, but, as a narrative poet, he always put in the what, where, and why of the things he was writing of. Bulletins delivered from the front of his consciousness in story-poems, close to prose, making use in some pieces of the old interview format of he said, she said, I said, and of "and" as connective tissue of his lineation. "he said, hell, you don't want a job,/ and I said, hell no but I need money,/and I finished the beer/and got on the bus…" ('looking for a job').

After college Hank moved out of his parent's house to live alone, and to become a writer, like those he admired: Saroyan, Hemingway, and John Fante among others.

JOHN FANTE

After his college days, Hank lived in a rooming house in John Fante's old neighborhood, Bunker Hill (torn down for Urban Renewal in the 1960's—pg. 55 Miles). Hank's mother bailed him out with money now and again and brought him clean underwear. He found temporary work—one of his jobs as laborer washing freight cars in the Southern Pacific Rail Road yard (pg. 56 Miles).

Buk thought of John Fante as his "god," and called Fante's novel ASK THE DUST (1939) "the finest novel written in all time" (pg. 9, Stephen Cooper, FULL OF LIFE, A Biography of John Fante). The poet Robinson Jeffers, by the way, Bukowski also called his "god."

Fante the writer, according to Barry Miles, was most responsible for Bukowski's writing style. According to another Bukowski biographer, Neeli Cherkovski, it was from Fante Buk learned the value of writing about the life in front of him—the quotidian world of day to day living.

John Fante was born in 1909, first of 4 children born to an immigrant couple of Italian heritage.

Like the father, Geremio, of Pietro di Donato's high-cholesterol novel CHRIST IN CONCRETE (Book-of-the-Month Club bestseller, 1939) and the father's paisanos, Fante's father Nick worked as a mason. The mother was religious and had considered joining the Catholic order of nuns before her marriage. The family resided on the North side of Denver, Colorado, until their relocation to Boulder, Colorado in 1915.

Early on in life, young John heard the epithet "Dago," and others (wop, guinea, etc.) thrown his way. The family, like many others, fell victim to the anti-foreigner, anti-Catholic, WASP majority and self-proclaimed hierarchy of citizens, and to the revitalized version of the Ku Klux Klan.

"Johnnie," small for his age, slept three to a bed, and grew up mostly out of doors, in a kind of Huck Finn (not Tom Sawyer) American childhood, free to roam unsupervised in rural surroundings. Johnnie was sent to Catholic School and eventually graduated from a Jesuit High School, Regis High. Though only 5'3" tall, Johnnie was a hard-nosed battler and a force to be reckoned with on the fields of play. He was also a boxer, punching his opponents so that he would not punch his abusive and philandering father. But the fight came anyway. In Johnnie's written account—related in his short story "Home Sweet Home" (pg. 47 Cooper) the Johnnie-like protagonist knocks his father down, and the old man begins to cry (Buk's dad merely gave up).

Before the end of his High School days, Fante had begun a shift from Catholicism toward Deism—reinforced by a growing skepticism in religious revelation and his identification with the ideas of Frederick Nietzsche.

Like Bukowski, Fante also took himself to the library where, in like manner, found his "gods." One being "The Baltimore Sage," critic and writer H. L. Mencken. The budding Nietzschean began an epistolary relationship with confirmed Nietzschean Mencken—a relationship that paid handsome dividends for Fante. Before any payment, however, young Johnnie tried college, which, again Bukowski-like, he did not remain at for long.

Meanwhile, the father Nick abandoned the family, leaving John de facto head of the household. After hitch hiking to Wilmington, California, Johnnie found employment at menial labor jobs, including work in a fish-cannery. His siblings and mother soon joined him (there were 3 Uncles living in the area as well).

Notably head-strong, pugnacious, and prone to violence, Fante appears to have suffered from some unspecified "little man's disease." The fighting spirit carried over to Fante's ambitions to become not just any old writer but a "great" writer. Toward this end, he returned to college at Long Beach Junior College in 1931. At the college an English teacher praised his writing. As a 23 year old freshman Fante had a short story accepted by H. L. Mencken for his magazine, "The American Mercury." Also, around this time, Fante—probably still a virgin, consummated a relationship with a woman ten years his senior.

After publication in Mencken's well-regarded and internationally known magazine, and, again dropping out of college, Fante made an impressive run for a twenty-four year old writer (for a writer of any age) by publishing half a dozen short stories in high-paying publications; signing a contract for a book with a New York publisher Knopf; and securing a job paying $250 weekly as script-writer for Warner Brothers Studio in Hollywood…All this during the heart of the depression years in America. (As meanwhile, in New York City, an impoverished writer named James T. Farrell, author of STUDS LONIGAN (1932-35) and other American naturalist classics, turned down $250 weekly from Metro-Goldwyn-Mayer Studios so that he could continue writing novels.)

Driven by over-weening ambition and self-centered pride, Fante gave the protagonist hero of his novels, Arturo Bandini, much of his own monstrous narcissism. In Fante's first novel, THE ROAD TO LOS ANGELES, Bandini, 18 years old, lives in Wilmington, California, and is a reader, like Johnnie, of Nietzsche, Schopenhauer, Kant, and Spengler. It is a book so funny it hurts. Rampant emotionalism tied to blatant literary hyperthyroidism. Loss of innocence the theme: like Herman Melville's young swabbie 'Redburn,' aboard the 'Highlander,' Bandini moves blindly and face-first into a reality at great odds with his understanding. Odds so large he seems an idiot (shades of Dana Hilliot, the sailor—the innocent of Malcolm Lowry's first novel ULTRAMARINE). Already a "great" writer, in his mind, Bandini is a scourge of the mediocrities (the boo-boo-zee). "A novel that lives," Fante biographer Stephen cooper wrote, "on the arid fumes of its own black humor." The book was posthumously published.

Fante and Joyce Smart, an ex-Stanford University graduate, and a poetess, met and fell in love and eloped to marry in 1937. Eloped because Joyce's family—her father a wealthy lumber merchant—disapproved of Johnnie, the wop from the wrong side of the tracks.

From an L. A. apartment, Joyce went to work for the W.P.A. (Works Progress Administration) while John finished another novel, this one finding a publisher. WAIT UNTIL SPRING BANDINI, 1938, was an "immortal work of art," Fante informed friend and fellow "writer-braggart" William Saroyan (pg. 153 Cooper).

Publication of the novel gave Fante some literary celebrity. He began work on another novel, a book which would be acclaimed his best, the now classic ASK THE DUST, 1939. Featuring, again, over-wrought and borderline manic-depressive Arturo Bandini. "A marvel of realistic urgency and poetic power" Fante biographer Stephen Cooper writes of the book. We know how highly Bukowski thought of it: from the Black Sparrow Press introduction, on the reissue of the novel: "at last…a man unafraid of emotion. Humor and…pain…intermixed with a superb simplicity."

Fante and Joyce were able, after the novel's publication, to afford a house on Manhattan Beach. A fallow period, writing-wise, for Fante followed, which included much drinking and a serious car accident (was it a suicide attempt? No one but Fante knew). John spent some serious time in the hospital, cooling his jets and writing, at leisure, a well-received book of short stories DAGO RED (1940).

Three published and critically praised books had not improved Fante's financial condition all that much as he was profligate with money, living the kind of life Bukowski's alter-ego character Henry Chinaski lived: drinking, fighting, gambling, and whoring. Fante's wife—certainly a candidate for sainthood, put up with his shenanigans and also urged John to stick with fiction-writing, and not movie scripts. The Fante's first child, however, was on the way and John bore-down on the

Hollywood assembly-line, writing a script for Paramount Pictures titled "Mrs. Wiggs of the Cabbage Patch," at $1000 clams a week.

By 1944 Fante's gambling problems, alcoholism, and absence from the home (he had become a golfing fanatic) put an even bigger strain on his wife's nerves, whose urging went ignored, Fante abandoning a 4th novel and continuing to write at the grist mill, as, in his words, a "Hollywood whore."

Around this period Fante had a spiritual conversion—or was it a confusion? He returned to the Catholicism of his childhood. Joyce also converted: She had previously been a Lutheran.

When his near-do-well father died, Fante made a show of grief, eulogizing the old man as honorable and manly, exemplified by the number of women the old reprobate conquered and number of fights he'd had (including one in which he'd nearly stabbed to death an opponent).

In a 1952 novel FULL OF LIFE Fante sentimentalized family life in a "benign sanitation" (pg. 288 Cooper). The novel made Fante $40,000: enough to buy a house in Malibu and move there with wife and four children in tow.

In what seems, to me, some sort of denial of reality, Fante wrote-up a television series based on the lives of Christian saints and became script-writer for the studios on stories of all manner of holy men and women who made it onto the silver screen.

It is possible, I think, that Fante lost his mind, which, ironically, would have put him in better stead in Hollywood—with other mindless purveyors of mush fed to audiences mindless themselves.

For $1500 weekly Fante served as in-house studio Catholic. He also continued living an increasingly fragmented and manic-depressive life-style. Diagnosed in '55 with diabetes, he paid little or no attention to dietary restrictions in treatment of the disease.

Years rolled by: Joyce immersed herself in spirituality: the Fante children grew up and left the nest; John fantasized about returning to the writing of serious fiction but wrote, instead, a mid-60's novel titled MY DOG STUPID, which went unpublished. He did become serious again in his 1970's novel THE BROTHERHOOD OF THE GRAPE, the "most mature and wisest" of Fante's novels according to Stephen Cooper. The book regained some interest in Fante from literary circles.

In the late 70's the bill for Fante's neglect of his health came due: amputation of toes, then a foot, then a leg. Plus diabetic retinopathy episodes bringing on periods of blindness. Also paranoid episodes with hallucinations, either from the disease or the treatment. Episodes that frightened Joyce, and no doubt John. His long Calvary had begun.

In the midst of John's continuous medical emergencies, Charles Bukowski made contact with Fante and reported that his, Bukowski's, publisher, Black Sparrow Press, was to reissue Fante's novel ASK THE DUST, out of print for thirty years. Bukowski claimed Fante the only living writer he admired. Writing in a poem ('the wine of forever') of Fante's "pure and magic emotions (hung) on the simple clean line." In a letter to Fante by Bukowski: "you mean more to me than any man living or dead" (pg. 155, CHARLES BUKOWSKI ON WRITING, Ed. Abel Dibretto).

Black Sparrow's subsequent reprints of most of Fante's novels, and the interest thereby engendered, moved John to dictate a final novel, DREAMS FROM BUNKER HILL, 1982, to his wife. DREAMS the last installment in the Arturo Bandini saga.

Fante died in the hospital at age 74. His a drawn-out horror movie-type death, his body disappearing piece by piece. Because of Buk's sponsorship and sales of Fante's reissued books, Joyce was made much more comfortable in her old age.

ON THE ROAD

After quitting, or being fired from any number of low-paying mostly temporary jobs in the Los Angeles area, Hank left his room and hit the road. His time spent traveling—as long as five years or short as two—has never been established. Stops on his itinerary included Miami, Atlanta, NYC, St. Louis, Philadelphia, San Francisco, Kansas City, and Chicago, but first stop for Hank was New Orleans. Arriving on a bus, and with his virginity still intact, he moved into a rooming house—one of many such houses he would occupy in his lifetime. Rooms where, he wrote, "you closed the door and there you were. The factory was gone, the warehouse was gone. Those…rooms were great places" (pg. 16, SELECTED LETTERS Vol 4, ed. Seamus Cooney, Letter to J. Martin). Such rooms were sanctuary. Rooms where Buk set his typewriter—if he had one (otherwise he hand-printed his work). The room would acquire a kind of holiness, like a grotto from which the poems and stories came (mostly stories at this time), and the typewriter holy too because it the vehicle from which the rapped-out work would emerge. A big clunky typewriter—a cast iron Remington the size of a lawn mower engine. Hard to lug around. Whenever he hit a key the table or desk as well as floor shook. Letters slapped down with machine gun staccato that woke the neighbors and the dead: the dead neighbors. One screaming "HEY KNOCK IT OFF!" and threatening to call cops ('these mad windows that lack life and cut me if I go through them').

I used a comparatively svelte manual but even that would make considerable noise, moving the woman who lived in the apartment below me to audibly sigh, heavily, exasperatedly, whenever I'd begin to type. I learned to balance the machine on my knees as I typed: a little crimped, but kept the peace between the neighbor and me…Bukowski, when living in an apartment on De Longpre Avenue in L.A. agreed to a ten p.m. cut-off time for typewriting, after multiple complaints from neighbors and the landlord.

Philadelphia was one of Hank's favorite cities—just behind New Orleans and Los Angeles. It was in the City of Brotherly Love that Hank first had sexual intercourse with a woman—a 300-pound whore he calls "Ann" in one of the newspaper columns he wrote for OPEN CITY (columns collected in NOTES OF A DIRTY OLD MAN, 1969). It was in Philly also, in '42, Hank was apprehended by the FBI for failing to register with the draft board. Hank spent 17 days in lock-up for the failure (pg. 63 Miles). Buk later claimed the stretch did not faze him; in fact, like a true Ubermensch, he rose above circumstances and managed to profit from his stay by beating fellow inmates at shooting dice. "ace-crapshooter, money man in a world of almost no money" Buk later wrote in his poem 'moyomeasing prison.' He would fictionalize his prison time in his short story 'Remember Pearl Harbor' published in his 1973 collection SOUTH OF NO NORTH.

While in the slammer Buk was sent to speak with a psychiatrist who stated that he was unfit for military service and tagged him 4-F, a "psycho-case."

A Ubermensch in action story, told by Buk in his 1975 novel FACTOTUM, is the story of his visit to a gangster-bar in Philly, where, after trying to pick-up the boss gangster's daughter, Chinaski (Buk's alter-ego) is black-jacked in the men's room, but refuses to leave, thus earning the admiration of the gangsters who ask him to join the gang.

Taking a beating is what Chinaski does best. He is the antithesis of the macho-man. Not starting fights, or seeking them out, but not backing down from any either. He is who Bukowski labeled the "Frozen Man." One who moves through life with feelings kept deep within, buried; a man who lives a distance apart from his feelings; one who cares but cannot seem to become incensed or joyous about things that matter so much to others, like patriotism, sports, political parties and philosophies, holidays…A man apart rather than alone, whose toughness consists of surviving, with style, the beatings he receives from others, such as his father, and from a society that routinely beats it's citizens into submission.

There is a kind of wisdom and even heroism, however reluctant, in such a stance. By not reacting, not joining, and not trying (DON'T TRY Bukowski had engraved on his tombstone) Chinaski declares his independence. By remaining non-affiliated and by not participating in certain ritualized tribal activities (voting, praying) he claims a kind of sovereignty onto himself.

What would Ernest Hemingway, a Bukowski hero, and Ubermensch par excellence, have done in the gangster bar? As epitome of macho, he would have cracked somebody's skull open. Or killed the gangster's pets; used his Mauser on the cats, dogs, parakeets, iguanas, goldfish, and the rest. (Buk liked the early-Hem, maker of the good clean line, "the true line devoid of ornament," (Buk wrote) but disliked the late-Hem of the fouled and humorless line.)

Bukowski took his beatings, as does his fictionalized self Chinaski, thereby demonstrating his endurance, and leaving with pride intact. Not such a heroic retreat but living to fight, or get beat, another day. While in St. Louis Hank received word of the acceptance of one of his short stories. By the prestigious STORY Magazine. Payment $25. Other publications followed: PORTFOLIO, Caresse Crosby's magazine, and MATRIX a Philadelphia-based publication.

Living without companionship, and hence, without being touched, except by prostitutes he could occasionally afford, Hank got his "touch" (which, as comedian Norm McDonald said, is how people know that they exist) through fistfights, like those entered into with Tommy the bartender (see BARFLY, the movie, 1987). The fights helped to remind Hank that he was, indeed, 'alive.' Also, by doing violence to another, he was not doing so to himself. The violence done Buk by his father got translated, it seems to me, by Hank's psyche into a form of communication, and even love. A perverse love. Perhaps the only "love" his father was capable of giving.

Hank returned home, to L. A., after, as I've said, an unspecified amount of time "on the road." He was greeted by his mother—not so much by the father. The old man told Hank that he would be charged for room & board and laundry. Hank stayed two years, leaving the house again in '47 and entering his so-called silent period: no writing, reportedly (by Hank), for ten years.

Hank moved into a room in downtown L. A. and into a Hollywood scene of whores, derelicts, strip joints, pawn shops, liquor stores, bars, X-rated theaters, and hock-shops—far from the "downtown" Petula Clark sang of.

Tarzan meets Jane in the neon jungle: Jane Cooney Baker, ten years Hanks' senior. A "looker" Bukowski called her. Chinsaski describes her as "firm-fleshed, almost beautiful." The two began living together in an apartment east of MacArthur Park (pg. 85 Miles). After a few weeks of drunk and disorderly conduct—Jane was, likewise, alcoholic, the pair were thrown-out and began a hegira through L. A. motel rooms and rooming houses.

Jane the first woman to give Hank much attention. Her attentions both motherly and mistress-ly. Hank fell in love. Whether Jane was likewise smitten is unknown to anyone but Jane, who continued to work casually as a prostitute. She was something of a will-of-the-wisp, making the most of opportunities that presented themselves. In his work, Bukowski often referred to her as "whore." In his poem 'fire station' Jane and the unnamed narrator, putatively Buk, visit a fire station, and while the narrator plays cards with the firemen, Jane takes on half a dozen at $5 a pop. In another Buk poem, 'I love you,' Hank, the pimp, scores another $5 leaving Jane with a man in a "dirty undershirt."

The couple's lifestyle continued as challenge to any landlord as well as less inebriated neighbors.

Jane, 38 years old when she and Hank met, was a daughter of a Saint Louis doctor who died when she was 9 years old (pg. 28 Sounes). Taking up drinking after the death of her husband, who died in a car crash at age 41, Jane became estranged from her two children and family of origin.

Hank worked unskilled laboring jobs to pay for rent and booze. Factory assembly-line worker, moving man, warehouseman, agricultural worker, shipping clerk….Jobs that paid little but demanded little responsibility either. Jobs to be had for the asking and not requiring (in these mid-century years) a resume or battery of interviews to be hired. Jobs described in Bukowski's novel FACTOTUM, 1975, a novel that, unlike Buk's first, POST OFFICE, 1967, written in a month, took Buk, reportedly, four years to complete. The book given impetus by Bukowski's reading of George Orwell's DOWN AND OUT IN PARIS AND LONDON (1933). Bukowski believed he could top Orwell's experience, as a bottom-feeder, with his own.

FACTOTUM

The story opens strongly, sinks somewhat in middle passages, then revives and redeems itself in spectacular fashion in final stages. Bukowski splits the underbelly of the world of unskilled labor wide open, affording readers a clear view.

A sub-title of the work could be the "Education of Henry Chinaski," a troubled soul and would-be writer who reaches, during his journey, something like profundity upon discovery that "everything is a hoax."

The name 'Chinaski' developed from Buk's early use of 'Chelaski'— encountered in Buk's 1946 short story "The Reason Behind Reason" (pg. XI, CHARLES BUKOWSKI, Absence of the Hero, Ed. D. S. Calonne.) 'Chelaski' derived from obvious similarity to Bukowski.

Buk's description of Chinaski's bosses are wonderfully succinct: "a tall man with no ass"—"a bald man with strange tuffs of hair over each ear." Some of the conversations Bukowski has Chisnaski carry-on are priceless miniature classics, like that between Chinaski and Maurice, the janitor in an Art Supply store; like that of Chinaski and Mrs. Farringlow in the Hotel Sands.

Chinaski moves city to city, job to job, each city and job more or equally absurd and meaningless to Chinaski—as his life seems, to him, likewise absurd and meaningless. Chinaski is the loner in extremis and is hated by the herd of his fellow workers because of his outsider status exemplified by what is perceived as an attitude of superiority to his work-mates. His refusal to conform or meet others' expectations—to get with the program—is a threat to the herd, who need conformity if they are to remain of the herd...Back in L. A. Chinaski meets his Venus, Laura, an aging blonde and a drunk, with shapely legs and can. The two pair-off but Laura soon fades from the picture as Grace, Jerry, Carmen, and Jan, Henry's shack-job (who sounds and acts suspiciously like Laura) come into view. The story takes an odd turn as Chinaski morphs into a Romeo of sorts and begins banging everything in sight, and what he cannot bang he drinks…The drinking—this is a story of drinking and working, leads Chinaski and his paramours into one jackpot after another, but never, in the novel, does anyone have a thought of quitting the booze, or of even slowing down: it is of the life, after all. And what a life! The booze makes for continuance of the drama, high and low.

Chinaski breaks from L. A. again to crawl back into the lower colon of the American dream. This time, to Miami where he finds the same dead-end jobs and people as previously encountered, in those other cities, where, like some kind of pilgrim, he bled and fell to his knees in drunken streets like someone doing penance before the stations of the cross.

Returning yet again to L. A., Henry shacks-up with Jan again. Jan is a whore but Henry is not bothered by that fact; she brings booze to him, and laughter, also the crabs…The drinking, whoring, and poor hygiene defy belief but Chinaski's work experiences feel real enough: the inanity of so much of it, workers and bosses—the system in general—the catalogue of beaten, desperate, resigned, and dull humankind in a tedious and repetitive Hell…One that our Virgil, Chinaski, navigates with all the style he can muster.

Only Buk's POST OFFICE among modern novels I've read is as good in describing not only the feel of the work itself but the environment too. (James T. Farrell's novel GAS-HOUSE MCGINTY, 1933, also contains a scrupulous look at those working for a living, including the rough speech and manners of working people brutalized by their occupation and the lives they lead outside of working hours. So too, THE LONELINESS OF THE LONG DISTANCE RUNNER, 1959, by Alan Sillitoe.) Except for the middle section, with Henry back in L. A. and treading water, FACTOTUM moves at a fervent pace, rolling along like a Greyhound bus out of L. A. Central Station.

GOING POSTAL

In 1950 Hank took a temporary position with the United States Post Office in L. A. By '52 he had become a regular postman delivering mail. He kept a job with the Post Office—as Postman and, later, Postal Clerk, for twelve years. Working usually 2nd or 3rd shift, and often required to do overtime, which meant eight to twelve-hour long shifts. As clerk he worked two straight weeks then had 4 days off. The clerks were forbidden to talk to each other while sorting the mail. (Richard Wright, American novelist, also worked as Postal Clerk, but in Chicago. Wright was another who could lay down the true unadorned line.) There were 3,000-plus workers in the L. A. Post Office annex, 900 N. Alameda Street—a majority of those workers non-Anglo.

One fine morning in 1955 thirty-five year old Hank began bleeding, from his mouth and rectally. Jane called for an ambulance and Hank was carted to the charity ward of L. A. General Hospital.

The piper had arrived, demanding the bill be paid.

Hank received 9 pints of blood and 8 of glucose (pg. 98 Miles) and was sent to the ward for the terminally-ill (where he refused offer of last rites from a Catholic priest). In future stories in which Hank told of his hospital stay he increased dramatically the number of pints: by 1971 the pints had risen to 13 (pg. 92, "Dirty Old Man Confesses," PORTIONS FROM A WINE-STAINED NOTEBOOK, Ed. D. S. Calonne).

Hank beat the percentages escaping the terminally-ill ward. After a three-day stay on the ward and a week elsewhere in the hospital he was discharged. And told, upon discharge, by a doctor, that if he, Hank, ever drank booze again the booze would most likely kill him. Hank heeded the warning, but because drinking had been so big a part of his previous days, he was clueless as to how to fill the hours of his new non-drinking life.

Jane suggested Hank investigate horse-racing and Hank did so. Soon, the race track became a fixture and kind of necessity to Bukowski. By going to the track, he went to the "people" but was not really of them; rather, an observer, an outsider (by choice) afforded a look at the madness of a race-track crowd. This tenuous connection became a tonic for Buk, allowing him, momentarily, to feel as if one of the people; the feeling gained while maintaining a certain distance, which he could close or lengthen, as he wished. Rubbing shoulders with the hoi polloi, but not having to hug one. "A man of the crowd," Barry Miles writes, "not man in the crowd."

Bukowski wrote that the track was a good place to hide, "like the bars used to be" ('if you slow down the mermaids look the other way'). Bukowski eventually became a sophisticated player—a student of horse-racing; an aficionado, and though he never wrote a full-length study, like Hemingway's bull-fighting text DEATH IN THE AFTERNOON (1932), Bukowski parsed-out the "sport of Kings" in poems and stories (particularly in "Picking the Horses" published in the L. A. Free Press, 1975, and reproduced, pg. 162-68, PORTIONS).

Hidden, though in plain sight, like Buk at the tract, was a strategy he also employed while in his apartment writing as he faced the street from the window. The access to whatever was happening outside was material he often incorporated in his work. A woman pushing a baby carriage, a man using a lawn mower, making his "gasoline sound" ('grass'), a girl in a red dress, a boy half the girl's size, all made it into the verse to be extrapolated upon, used, in the work and without his having to take part in the action—able to remain observer, at a distance: the distance necessary to him as artist in maintaining the objectivity to do his work justice.

After his discharge from the hospital Buk claimed he felt different, "calmer," as he told a friend, than previous to his admission. Surviving

Big Daddy Death seemed to have changed Hank on some psychic level. Barry Miles suggests a "transcendent experience" of some kind. Maybe because of the change, or coincidental to it, Hank began to write in earnest again, but strictly poetry, claiming the stuff came out of him almost automatically, as if dictated, while he sat at the "typer" in a near trance-like state. (Henry Miller, during his writing of TROPIC OF CAPRICORN, 1939, claimed a "voice" spoke the words to him that he subsequently wrote down.)

Jane asked Hank to move out after her daughter showed up unexpectedly, and pregnant. Hank complied.

Bukowski began an epistolary romance with a poetess and editor (of Harlequin Magazine) who lived in Texas. Barbara Frye was eleven years Hank's junior. She had been born missing two neck vertebrae, which confined the movement of her head; she also had a slightly curved spine, but otherwise quite able. She told Hank, after they were married— because Barbara insisted on a marriage license before any sex to be had—following their whirlwind courtship, she was a nymphomaniac.

Barbara was, unofficially, the 3rd woman Hank had sexual congress with—calling into question all the sexual exploits he'd written of earlier in poems and stories.

The couple set-up house in Brandon Street in Echo Park, an L. A. suburb, "a little run down" (pg. 109 Miles); a working class neighborhood occupied mostly by a non-Anglo population.

In Hank's novel POST OFFICE, Barbara, as 'Joyce,' is described as a "nymph" who could "cook better," Chinaski says, "than any woman he'd ever known."

Hank later wrote of servicing his new wife at least eleven times a week. Barbara soon began to realize that she had gotten more than she'd bargained for in Hank. Living with an alcoholic, she discovered, was no walk in the park. Also, she wanted a bourgeois life, like the one she lived in Texas; a life that did not seem to interest Hank, though, I suspect, he certainly would have accepted one, so long as he did not have to put in an inordinate amount of work to get it.

To Barbara, Hank's habit of lying around the house and drinking beer and reading the Racing Form hinted at a lack of ambition. The differences in temperament—he thought her something of a snob and princess—became too wide to breach and Barbara moved-out (leaving Hank her car).

A hilarious account of this mis-coupling can be found in POST OFFICE.

The marriage lasted 2 years and 4 months.

Hank also moved, into an apartment on Mariposa Avenue, which he kept for the next six years. A divorce was granted in 1958.

After the divorce Hank encountered Jane again ('Betty' in POST OFFICE) who, Hank realized, had rapidly aged as well as grown heavier. They tried to reunite but it did not work for Hank who felt something missing—a space between them. He started to pity her, and concluded a poem about the attempt to reunite, with "we both had been robbed." Jane drank herself to death in 1962. Hank wrote many poems about Jane, including a number of poems on her death, many published in his 1969 collection THE DAYS RUN AWAY LIKE WILD HORSES OVER THE HILL. In 'for Jane with all the love I had which was not enough' the poet revisits the scene of the hotel room where his paramour—who worked as a chambermaid, had died. "I pick up the skirt,' he wrote, "all her loveliness gone,/and I speak to the gods/but /they will not give her back to me." (This strong Bukowski collection also features poems about the birth and liveliness of his daughter—the daughter born in 1964. The engaging and loveable interactions between poet and daughter lift the atmosphere somewhat after the poems of eulogy.)

In 1960 the editor of HEARSE Magazine, one E. V. Griffth published a chapbook of 16 poems by Bukowski, titled FLOWER, FIST, AND

BESTAIL WAIL, a title alluding to D. H. Lawrence's BIRDS, BEASTS, AND FLOWERS (pg. 55, D.S Calonne, CHARLES BUKOWSKI, Critical Lives). Buk, at the time, was 40 years old. The publication was a milestone for him. According to Jules Smith, Bukowski paid half of the book's printing cost (pg. 50, Jules Smith, ART, SURVIVAL, AND SO FORTH).

Editors of a New Orleans-based magazine called 'The Outsider," edited by the Webbs, John and Gypsy Lou, began to publish Buk's poems and to champion his work, putting Bukowski's picture on the cover of an issue and calling him "Outsider of the Year." Buk rode a bus to New Orleans to participate in the Webb's production of the Bukowski title IT CATCHES MY HEART IN ITS HANDS. The work an artsy production: 777 printed copies hand-bound on fancy paper (pg. 134, Miles). Bukowski was paid in copies of the book (pg. 80 Sounes).

Buk's work also began appearing in EVERGREEN Review, a well-respected, and paying publication, begun by Grove Press in 1957 (continued to 1984, ceased, and returned as online publication in 1988, then again in 2017) as well as in lesser known, and less-paying, Indie or "little" magazines.

In a round-about fashion Buk hooked-up with one Francis Elizabeth Dean, an ex-graduate of Smith College, poetess, and divorced mother of four children. At the time of their meeting, Francis was depressed over the failure of her marriage and subsequent loss of her children. She moved from the East coast to East Hollywood to be closer to Bukowski. Beginning to call herself FrancEyE, and living with Bukowski, she became pregnant at 41 years old. The baby girl, named Marina, was born while Buk and FrancEye lived in a unit of De Longpre Avenue, south of Sunset Boulevard (pg. 140 Miles).

FrancEyE began the relationship viewing Bukowski as some kind of father-figure, a "very solid person underneath lots of bluster" she told Neeli Cherkovski (pg. 137 Cherkovski, BUKOWSKI, A Life), who also notes that during the war Francis joined the WAC's, looking on the Army as an all-embracing "father" (pg. 135, Cherkovski). Buk became irritated by what he called FrancEyE's "groupism"—her attachment to poetry workshops and to like-minded political and social "friends." Irritated by her "prattling" voice as well. In a letter to Doug Blazeck, one of Buk's favored 60's and 70's correspondents, Buk writes that FrancEyE is "dead" and "will always be dead, but I must live with her because of the child" (pg. 159, SCREAMS FROM THE BALCONY, Selected Letters, 1960-70, Ed. Seamus Cooney).

FrancEyE's intuition, if that what it was, proved solid; despite some serious personal hang-ups, and his callous treatment of some, Buk was, by many accounts, a caring and tender father who fawned over his daughter.

In Bukowski's novel POST OFFICE FrancEyE is 'Fay,' a writer "of some sort" says Chinaski, who lives off of alimony checks from ex-hubby and money sent by her mother. The section of the novel telling the story of Marina's birth is the most touching and tender part of that book.

The time came when it was necessary, once again, for Hank to leave L. A. and travel to New Orleans. The Webb's were putting out another book of Bukowski's poems. Hank rode the Sunset Limited out of Union Station (pg. 144 Cherkovski). Arrived in the Crescent City, Hank was put-up in a house in the French Quarter, belonging to a woman-friend of the Webbs. "in New Orleans/I was living with/a fat woman" ('the spider'). The new book to be titled CRUCIFIX IN A DEATH HEAD—which became part of Buk's 1974 Selected Poems, BURNING IN WATER DROWNING IN FLAME. 3100 copies of DEATH HEAD were printed (pg. 150 Cherkovski).

Buk's writing, by this period, had a conspicuous presence in the "little" magazines. Lit mags of the "mimeo-revolution" like 'Ole,' 'Wormwood Review,' 'The Outsider,' 'Harlequin,' 'Quixote,' and other low-circulation zines that separated the wheat from the chaff. The wheat included, besides Buk, Doug Blazek, Steve Richmond, William Wantling, John Webb, Al Purdy, Harold Norse, and others (Anne Menebroker, Kaja)…Some of whom published work in Hank and Neeli's short-lived (3 issues) publication 'Laugh Literary and Man the Humping Guns.' In 1967 Buk considered Purdy and Norse the two "best living poets" (pg. 315 SCREAMS. Letter to Carl Weissner. Some of the best Bukowski letters went to Weissner.)

By '64 Bukowski was, again, heavily into the sauce: full-blown alcoholism. Vomiting each morning and maintaining a BAC high enough to keep him from going into shock or seizure or detoxification. In typical "denial" Buk said he was not an alcoholic because he could stop drinking IF he wanted to—and he did stop, a number of times and for a variety of reasons BUT could never stay stopped. He armored the denial with the fact of his functioning: as poet and prose writer he continued to be productive even while drinking heavily. That he did produce so much for so long and at such a high quality is a medical mystery—perhaps a miracle. The human body is a remarkable machine; also, I suspect Buk exaggerated the amounts drunk and had many "dry" periods, which did not warrant mention in his writings because he had trapped himself, in a sense, by the myth he'd created: the persona of the Ubermensch, who drank more, fought harder, fucked oftener, and lived more intensely than pretty much everyone or anyone else. Image of the tough guy brawler and hard drinker who took names while he kicked ass needed to be maintained to fit the created persona. Anecdotal evidence suggests the persona got dropped, or at least occasionally shed, in private. After Buk sold Henry Miller 3 copies of DEATH HEAD, Miller, who preferred wine to beer and hard liquor, gave Hank some advice: "drink only when you're happy IF YOU CAN, NEVER drown your sorrows and never alone!" (pg. 144 Miles). Advice that Hank, like any good alky, ignored. Hank drank when happy, sad, or indifferent. He drank while writing, he claimed; claimed to be indebted to the booze for making him able to write—helping to unleash his creativity. (Told that alcoholism is a "disease" Bukowski replied that everything is a "disease." Given a suggestion to go to Alcoholics Anonymous, he refused, saying that AA's 12 Steps to Recovery promoted a return to infancy—AA'er's would say "maturity.")

In November of '64 Buk had another hemorrhage and returned to the hospital. "My whole insides had fallen apart" he wrote Doug Blazeck (pg. 116 SCREAMS). "Friday, coughed-up a half pint of blood."

Hank took infrequent trips to the L. A. drunk tank (N. Avenue 21, Lincoln Heights) as well. His outre behavior, while drunk, alienated friends—like the Webbs, and he personally suffered the thousand cuts of the damned by falling down, walking on broken glass, having fist fights, and meeting with "accidents." All the usual self-damaging ways drunks maim their selves.

Hank also went into the hospital around this period for an operation on his hemorrhoids, and to have some of his lower intestines removed. He also split from his girlfriend, or she split from him. "Fay" splits from Chinaski in POST OFFICE, but according to Bukowski biographer Howard Sounes, Bukowski told FrancEyE to leave (pg. 76 Sounes). The separation was agreeable to each and child-support payments, which Buk faithfully sent, paying $45 monthly in '72—the amount "volunteered" by Buk (pg. 153, LIVING ON LUCK, Selected Letters, 1960-1970, Vol. 2, Ed. Seamus Cooney. Letter to Patricia Connell).

One fine day in 1966 a man named John Martin, manager of an office furniture and supply company as well as dealer in rare books— also a Christian Scientist and teetotaler, showed up at Bukowski's door. "Balding and red-headed," with "high scrubbed forehead…and a perpetual grin," Bukowski described Martin (intro. To BURNING IN WATER). Martin had read Bukowski's poems published in The OUTSIDER and requested to read more. Bukowski gave him access to a pile of unpublished verse and Martin left with a handful. Thus began Black Sparrow Press and Martin and Bukowski's long serendipitous collaboration. (From the handful of poems Martin printed broadsides to sell to collectors.) AT TERROR STREET AND AGONY WAY was the first Bukowski title published by the press. Called a "glorified chapbook" by Howard Sounes (pg. 88 Sounes), the work sold out the first printing of 875 copies (pg. 191 Cherkovski). Unlike the Webbs, Martin paid Bukowski royalties: $460 (pg. 330, SCREAMS). Martin also offered Hank $100 a month for life; a sum to be given whether Hank continued to send work to Black Sparrow or not. (So the story, which could be apocryphal, is told.)

Bukowski gladly accepted Martin's offer; he knew his days at the Post Office were numbered; his absentee record had brought he and the P. O. to a terminus. Buk had money socked away, from sale of his deceased parent's home (plus small checks from lit magazines, as well as a $5000 settlement from the P. O. after he retired (pg. 19, Smith). Yet, giving up his job was a big gamble. The financial insecurity raised by his leaving sent him into a tizzy, and a couple of drunken weeks face to face with the unknown future. An insecurity that can paralyze, and did, until Bukowski found it within himself to begin working in earnest despite his fears.

The resulting effort produced a novel, POST OFFICE, which Buk claimed to have written in a month.

Martin, reportedly, did not like the rawness of the work (pg. 179 Miles) and edited it for grammatical correctness. Buk reluctantly agreed to cuts (not made to a later, German-language, edition).

POST OFFICE

Henry Chinsaski, lumpen and prole, carries the weight of this short, 200 page, episodic novel. "Chinaski," Buk's alter-ego protagonist, had appeared previously in a Bukowski chapbook, published by Doug Blazeck's press, titled CONFESSIONS OF A MAN INSANE ENOUGH TO LIVE WITH BEASTS, a mini-autobiography in nine sections.

The novel has a little bit of everything in it: toughness and tenderness, passion and despair, humor and sadness, triumph and defeat. Chinaski has never strut with as much authority and elan as he does in this book.

Chinaski works at the L. A. Post Office and is in a sort of WAR ALL THE TIME (title of Buk's '84 poetry collection) to stay afloat, at the job and in the world. To live life—even just to exist—and work simultaneously, is a good trick, if you can pull it off without losing your sanity. The unemployment line, nut house, jail, and morgue are never far away for Chinaski, who walks a tightrope through the dangers. Of necessity, he puts up with Post Office bureaucratic chicken-shit plus intimidation of the "soups," supervisors, like the over-officious aptly named "Jonstone," whom Chinaski calls "Stone." The bosses "with bad breath/big feet/who look like frogs, hyenas…Who walk as if melody had never been invented": puts up with fellow workers as well, some of whom have become like robots on the assembly line of a robotic system designed without regard for those who keep the thing functioning: the workers.

Our anti-hero Chinaski, caught in the spokes of routine and repetitiousness of the Post Office Moloch fights to keep his mind from surrendering, or imploding, into the dullness of a narcotized death-in-life.

Chinaski's attitude toward the company and exploitative wage-slavery system is similar to that of "Henry Miller" the persona of TROPIC OF CAPRICORN (1939), who is out to screw the company he works for—the "Cosmodemonic Cocksucking Corporation"—before or while being screwed by it. An attitude in revolt against the cold anti-humanistic system of profit and loss, known as Capitalism. A humanism antithetical to the "bottom line" of business as business.

Whenever Chinaski calls-out sick, the company sends a nurse to his door to verify illness. The company is like Big Daddy, or Big Brother, in striving to infantilize the workers thereby making them easier to control. (Bukowski's empathy for the workers and other bottom-feeders in the system is a notable and laudable aspect of his work.)

The load on Chinaski's mail route is so heavy as to preclude his taking lunch, if he is to finish his assigned tasks in the allotted time and thereby keep his job. Time is not only of the essence, it is the essence. Hours and minutes are the brutal calculous regulating each employee's existence. Ten minute breaks—two every 8 hours—mean 10 minutes, no more. Chinaski's anarchic soul rebels: He steals minutes like a thief snatching jewels. The thieving has immediate consequences: Henry is "written-up" time after time. He appeals some of the chicken-shit Post Office decisions—like the one to remove half the water fountains from the building, to his Union rep, but the rep can only empathize not change anything…Chinaski's failure to get in lock-step and march as the others do soon has him up on the chopping block. He stands atop the block for almost twelve years, until conditions of his life change and he is, as we shall see, able to resign and thus escape the P.O.

POST OFFICE affirms the old common knowledge that working for a living will kill you, and not working for a living will do the same. To Bukowski, endurance was the important, vital, thing in life. To endure, with a sense of style and humor, is a special thing: Bukowski's GINGER MAN, Chinaski, does both (title J P Donleavy novel, 1955).

POST OFFICE is Bukowski's classic work; his response to Fante's ASK THE DUST and Hamsun's HUNGER (1890).

(Bukowski called Knut Hamsun "the world's greatest writer.")

OUT OF THE FRYING PAN AND INTO THE STOVE

In 1967 Buk became a columnist for OPEN CITY an underground L. A. newspaper. Buk's column, NOTES OF A DIRTY OLD MAN, ran for 82 weeks and made "Bukowski" a recognized name in L. A. He became something of a cult figure because of the column, which he was paid $10 weekly to produce (pg. 186 BUKOWSKI ON WRITING, Ed. Abel Debritto).

The editor of OPEN CITY labeled Bukowski an "asshole" but a great asshole. An opinion the editor altered, after feeling personally betrayed by Bukowski, to "great writer but lousy human being."

"So easy to be a poet," Bukowski wrote in his poem '40,000 flies' but "so hard to be a man."

The editor, John Bryan, believed that Bukowski did not like Bukowski very much—which is somewhat evident in Buk's self-destructive acts while drunk or hung-over. Bryan also seems, unfortunately, to have taken Bukowski's provocations seriously rather than in Buk's spirit of mocking satire (such as his assessment of the newspaper staff of long-hairs as "scummy commie hippies"). Bryan's nickname for Bukowski was "Bullshitski" (pg. 93, Sounes).

Meanwhile, the Post Office, which Bukowski was still employed by at this time, got wind of his OPEN CITY column—he'd used it to attack the P.O., and called Hank onto the carpet for a ream-job, threatening him with dismissal for 'Conduct Unbecoming a Postal Employee.' Hank responded with a threat to go to the ACLU and elsewhere, and refused the P. O.'s suggestion that he resign. (The P. O. not the only organization following Buk's doings: the FBI had opened a Bukowski file. Pg. 235, MORE NOTES OF A DIRTY OLD MAN, Ed. D. S. Calonne).

The columns were sold, for a $1000 advance against royalties, to a "porno" publisher and published in book form, as NOTES OF A DIRTY OLD MAN, in 1969. 20,000 copies quickly sold (pg. 212 Cherkovski).

1969 was a big year for Buk. The year Penguin Books included Bukowski's work in Penguin's prestigious 'Modern Poet's' series of books. Buk's work had been championed to Penguin editors by veteran poet Harold Norse. Norse, a gay man, became a good friend of Bukowski, but, like so many of Bukowski's friends, felt personally betrayed by something Buk wrote, and cooled on the relationship. Norse claimed that Bukowski misbehaved and ruined friendships to confirm feelings of "self-hatred" (pg. 172 Miles) and to push away intimacy that he, Buk, "will never," Norse wrote, "get in touch with." Fellow poet Doug Blazeck theorized that, in his letters, Buk could be vulnerable, intimate, and revealing, but only because he was at a safe distance: "he wanted to share love" wrote Blazeck, "but couldn't allow himself that luxury having been hurt so much in the past" (pg. 88 Sounes). In the same vein, Linda King, a Bukowski girl-friend of the 70's, believed "love" something Bukowski could not trust and therefore drove people away before any love had a chance to fail him (pg. 237 Cherkovski). In a Bukowski letter of 1965, to fellow poet William Wantling, he wrote "love is—only a form of selfishness" (pg.208 SCREAMS). In the flesh, Bukowski was often found wanting, lacking the warmth he exuded in his correspondence. Wantling and the Webbs were both crudely satirized by Buk in L.A. FREE PRESS columns. Vicious payback for their kindnesses. Though Chinaski may have been a generous soul as Buk's fictional Ubermensch, Bukowski himself was not. Case in point: after Wantling's death at a relatively young age (from his drug usage) his widow paid Buk a visit. Buk demanded sex from the grieving widow, reminding her that hubby was dead and could no long "suck her pussy," but that he, Buk, the Ubermensch, could (pg. 138 Sounes).

"An alcoholic in his cups," it is written in the BIG BOOK of Alcoholics Anonymous, "is an unlovely creature."

'69 was also the year Bukowski made Carl Weisser a part of his life. The German Weisser, a Fulbright scholar who had lived as a student in the U.S., before returning to Germany, was a poet and performance artist; he became translator of Bukowski's work, putting Bukowski before the German public. Weisser became, in time, Bukowski's European agent as well.

NOTES OF A DIRTY OLD MAN

Included in these collected columns is plenty of material that found its way into Bukowski's novels FACTOTUM and WOMEN (1978).

NOTES one of the first Bukowski titles I read: it sucked me into the orbit of Buk's writing; I found the stuff addicting and wanted more of it, and faster. An analogy to the viewing of pornography could be made here: I think I will make it—

As a seventeen year old construction laborer, during the summer before I went to my first college, I used to occasionally look, during down time in the shop, at the girly magazines stacked in a corner of the office where we took lunch-break. Looking through a magazine then picking up another, flipping the pages progressively faster, until reaching the end of one magazine then immediately grabbing another one, and, flip-flop, ever faster; looking faster you might say, gobbling the images with my eyes—all pleasure long gone in favor of multiplication of images—chasing the initial thrill (long since passed) like a junky after his or her fix.

I do not consider most of Bukowski's work pornographic because even in the stories he wrote for sex-magazines the sex is always secondary to the story. There is a lot more going on in the story than sex. It could be said that the sex is incidental to the story. There are exceptions, unfortunate exceptions, as in parts of WOMEN and in pieces such as 'Workout' a story written for HUSTLER Magazine (republished in PORTIONS). In these and certain other episodes Buk is as boringly gauche as any other hack pornographer writing for a dollar a page ("clichéd copulation," as Nabokov wrote of pornography). It is embarrassing to read a great writer prostituting his or her craft. Everyone, of course, has to make a living, and how it is done is a matter of choice and circumstance. OPUS PISTORUM, by example, reportedly written by Henry Miller, and referred to as a work of pornography is, certainly—if Miller did indeed write the thing (he denied doing so) a dark stain on his reputation.

NOTES contains a certain amount of journalese—pieces, after all, written to make a deadline. Buk's concern was not only making art but with the act of creation, mainly writerly concerns for narrative. He was also, obviously, concerned with entertainment value of his work, and the telling of some brutal truths along the way. His view of art, or, the Art World as such, is often derisive, referring to such as phonies playing a con-game of century's long duration. He spent a lot of energy puncturing the pompous and pretentious and had a raging disdain for writers and poets of a certain circumambient style, such as that of William Faulkner whom Buk called "the fraud of the century" and Malcolm Lowry whose writings Buk considered too "fancy" and "inbred."

In his work Buk cut out the chase, aiming straight for the heart, or elsewhere. In NOTES Buk's imaginative capacities are at full throttle: his story of the baseball player who grows wings does not work for me but his story of the man who turns green with gold specks does. One zany and outre piece after another, until, toward the book's end, more journalistic-type efforts appear.

"Callow journalism" wrote the N Y Times reviewer (pg. 147 Sounes). Gay Brewer, author of CHARLES BUKOWSKI (Twayne's United States Author Series, 1997) criticized the hip unconventionality of Buk's style—such as use of lower case letters throughout, as "distract(ing) from the powerful content" (pg. 47 Brewer)

In any case, Buk's voice, wry, trenchant, and easily recognizable—like Saroyan's, brought people to poetry and literature who previously had no interest in the medium. Buk's work expanded the perimeters of the genres, poetry and prose, to include those outside the arena—those who had only the most marginal interest in such doings. He helped democratize poetry and prose in America and elsewhere.

Hank met Linda King in 1970 and began the most tempestuous female-male relationship of his life. 1970 was also, he wrote, "the most magic year of my life" (pg. 112, LIVING ON LUCK, letter to J. Martin). Linda both sculptress and poetess and, reportedly, a "wild woman" who previously to meeting Bukowski had spent time in a nut house. Linda was not afraid to call Buk out on his B.S. "You care how Charles

Bukowsi feels, you don't care that much for anyone else," Linda wrote Bukowski (pg. 115 Sounes). Hank was smitten by her; so much so he went on the wagon to please her and stayed on 3 months—his weight subsequently dropping from 240 to 160 lbs. (pg. 188 Miles).

Divorced and with two kids, Linda liked action of all kinds. Hank had trouble keeping up with her. She thought him a Puritan and set out to teach him a few things about love & sex. Their relationship was full of high and low drama, the drama consisting sometimes of knock-down drag-out fights. He punched her and broke her nose. She blackened his eyes and shred his face with her fingernails; she once tried to run him over with her Volkswagen. Buk biographer Miles reports 40 or more break-ups during their first year together. Linda later said she did not accept, did not want, the kind of love Bukowski gave: "obsessive not natural" (pg. 114 Sounes).

THE 70'S SHOW

Worry about his slipping back into wage-earner status drove Buk to seek income through writing for the "sex" magazines. He also accepted a grant from the National Endowment for the Arts (pg. 76, Smith). He made additional money through giving poetry readings—work that he claimed to despise. In L. A. venues Buk attracted for larger crowds than the usual turn-outs for such events. During the readings and afterward Buk often played the clown—played Bukowski 'the dirty old man'—behavior he thought people expected of him. The expectations casting him into a persona that his mythomaniac writings had established.

A substantial Bukowski poetry collection appeared in print in '72, titled MOCKINGBIRD WISH ME LUCK.

From the window life presents itself: a dark girl reading the Bible, a smoking car, a boiling cloud on the horizon…All fodder for the poetry written by the man in the window. A woman with huge buttocks jammed into black slacks becomes transferred onto the page, like an act of magic. This is why, the poet writes, he is "God."

Jokey riffs of language; little episodes writ large; walking out of the dark into the dark, sitting, waiting…Ad hominin attacks on fellow poets, such as Steve Richmond. Excursions of the imagination, imagery plucked from the edge, the corner, of reality. The common made to serve the bizarre and uncanny: made to serve art. "Crystal clear snapshots," Bukowski critic Abel Debritto wrote, "of immediate experiences as well as the world at large" (pg. viii, ESSENTIAL BUKOWSKI, Ed. Abel Debritto).

Major poems that helped establish Bukowski's reputation: 'mockingbird,' 'hogs in the sky,' 'the last days of the suicide kid,' 'the rat,' 'the shoelace'…Linda King break-up poems, Linda love-poems, Linda boiling-in-oil poems…Marina poems (the daughter), death of a composer poem…Solid, substantial…

Bukowski is the disinterested American. The one who does not like holidays or parades or NASCAR racing or elections; is not a mover or shaker or go-getter in the commonly understood sense of those terms; no club affiliations except to barrooms, no bowling league (even Hitler bowled!), no political party membership. No ambition in the sense of trying to get ahead in the system—only ambition to work at his art. He is an 'other' to Babbitry's George: neither a join-er or josher, by heck-a-lorum. He is a sly saboteur who doesn't buy into the American myth: he sees the trap of prisons everywhere, and is wary, so wary, of "the aridity of/the ACTUAL/dream" ('darkness').

Linda is "Lydia" in Buk's 1978 novel WOMEN. The work edited by Martin who said his editing was an attempt to make the work "more literate" (pg. 225 Miles). Published previous to WOMEN was Buk's poetry collection LOVE IS A DOG FROM HELL, 1977, a "parallel text to WOMEN" (pg. 221 Miles).

LOVE IS A DOG FROM HELL

Bukowski's search for love and sex led him to encounters with a horde of women, many of whom nameless to history and therefore anonymous. A "Sandra" and "Scarlet" appear in the poems but others merely carry a label: 'platinum blonde,' "the Texan,' 'lady with a large bed,' '6 foot goddess,' and 'a groupie.'

Gone for the most part from the collection are the big field-sized lyrical pieces of earlier collections, in favor of terse, clipped, and the more succinct language of Buk's later minimalist and mature style.

The work is not really about women per se; it is primarily about the poet, the big "I." His scrotum and dick (his "string"); the state of his underwear (not good); state of his room: yellow walls, dirty sheets, cockroach in the sink; the state of his mind, or condition of his condition, such as "hung-over and a hard-on, and no lawyer" ('trapped'). The challenges of the nights too, when alone—despite all the women—and a small army of them march through the book—and pining for a touch, willing to trade all of his poems for a girl beside him in the dark.

In the ennui of some dull days, when the woman are absent, or are dull themselves, poetry leaks out, like from a leaky faucet: "headless in the night…eels climbing the bathroom walls…purple housewife's in the market fingering avocados…" Poems concerning 'Scarlet," described as red-headed, golden, and slightly ditzy—a description of a Bukowski girlfriend, main-squeeze of the late 70's, Pamela O'Brien aka 'Cupcakes' ('Tammy' in WOMEN). A voluptuous pill-taker and heart-breaker, and former "part-time hooker" Buk wrote in a letter to A.D. Winans (pg.222 LIVING ON LUCK). She accompanied Buk to New York City where he read at the Saint Marks Church project. Scarlet rates a dozen poems in the volume, while Linda, Katherine, Nina, and Irene, occupy one and the same poem. Jane also is subject of a poem.

Outside the poet's sanctum of room come the sounds of life in L. A., the brutal city. A "jungle of hot siren-whining nights," Kerouac wrote in ON THE ROAD (1957). Gunshots, and womp womp of helicopter blades overhead; and the neighbors, some of whom make too much noise, or the wrong kinds of noises...And knocks at the door, from women or perhaps a poet—"the sickest and lowest of the breed" ('my comrades'), subjects of Buk's parodic and satirical screeds—so too himself, his self-deprecatory stance adding humor and a dash of humility to his King status as Ubermensch.

The collection suffers the same defect as the novel WOMEN, which is—I quote Gay Brewer: "overwrought...and with a damaging lack of aesthetic distance" (pg. 123, Brewer).

When Linda King left the area to return to Utah where she was from, Buke replaced her with Liza, 'Dee Dee Bronson' in WOMEN, an executive in the music/recording industry and a popular figure in the underground newspaper scene. She too, as Buk, had written a column for the L. A. Free Press (pg. 242 Cherkovski). Liza drove a Mercedes and lived in an expensive Hollywood Hills house. Her love for Hank was not fully reciprocated, Buk placing bets elsewhere, including an epistolary romance with a 27 year old airline stewardess.

After telling Liza that he was going to Utah to visit Linda, Liza tried to overdose from sleeping pills. "Why do you need a bad woman?" she asks Hank ('I'm in love'). "You need to be tortured don't you? You want to be treated like a piece of shit—"

Meanwhile, City Lights Books published Buk's prose work ERECTIONS, EJACULATIONS, EXHIBITIONS, and General Tales of Ordinary Madness. (CITY LIGHTS Books picked up all the material of Buk's that John Martin was loathe to publish, disliking much of Buk's more blatantly sexual stuff.) This the book I bought from the Harvard Coop bookstore: The book with the ravaged face of Bukowski on the cover—a face that made me less self-conscious about the amount of pimples on my own face.

After Linda King returned from Utah to L. A. to live, she and Hank set up house in the L. A. suburb Silver Lake (pg. 193 Miles). Hank agreed not to drink in the house (how about in the yard?). Their relationship was an "open" one in that both took other partners. Linda the more tolerant, reportedly, of Buk's philandering; tolerant also of the "creepy, ugly, cockroach slime who inhabited," she said, "a drunken Bukowski" (pg. 198 Miles). Buk, holding onto the old double standard, went into a rage of jealousy whenever Linda stepped-out on him. "With obsessive love comes jealousy," Howard Sounes noted (pg. 114 Sounes).

Linda's poems which were, are, quite good, were published alongside those of Hank's in a chapbook. To some, Linda was "Bukowski with a cunt" (pg. 197, Miles).

WOMEN

The original title of this novel was LOVE TALES OF THE HYENA. The novel sold more copies than any other Bukowski novel (pg. 185 Sounes). Bukowski reportedly used the form of Boccaccio's THE DECAMERON as template for his book. John Martin and Buk did quite a bit of sparring over the novel's contents, Buk telling Martin that he did not want his writing SMOOTHED out or his wordage changed so much that the changes disturbed the natural flow of the writing (pg. 151, BUKOWSKI ON WRITING. Ed. Abel Dibretto. Letter to Carl Weissner). "You imagine him (Martin) touching up a Van Gogh?" Buk wrote. ('Touching up' became Martin's thing in Bukowski posthumous publications.)

The novel records the poet's search for sex and love, through the pursuit of a horde of women. Linda, "Lydia," pops Chinaski's blackheads as they lie in bed: Lydia suddenly sits up and announces that she is going to be GREAT. Also, that she has seen God. She screams (she's a screamer) then starts to beat on Henry, beside her. He flees to Dee Dee (Liza) a lady executive, and her home in Hollywood Hills. Henry tells Dee Dee not to fall in love with him. But she is soon smitten. Henry thinks, Arturo Bandini-like, of Nietzsche: contemplates himself as a German stallion to Dee Dee's Jewish mare...After Henry tells Dee Dee that he is returning to Lydia, Dee takes an overdose of pills, but does not croak. Henry leaves to visit Lydia who is like a drug Henry is addicted too. Meanwhile, Nicole, a cultured broad, sends a letter Hank receives. He responds with a visit, arriving at her place in an alcoholic black-out. He screws the "culture bitch" while telling himself that, Swinburne-like, he is being "faithful to thee (Lydia) in my fashion." Right. Lydia does not agree and attacks Nicole...Mindy comes on board, from NYC. A "looker" with style. Henry is on her like white on rice. "Sex" he thinks, "is like one animal knifing another into submission."

Lydia attacks Mindy also. Mindy exits (falls on sword, dies). Laura, whom Henry thinks resembles Katherine Hepburn, the movie star, shows up at a Chinaski poetry reading and Henry afterward beds-her. She invites him to Texas. An acquaintance of Laura/Katherine, one 'Joanna,' a 6-footer, shows up at Hank's apartment. He beds her too, even though he thinks he may be falling in love with Laura/Katherine. When Laura/Katherine also visits, Henry slips her the old wiener-schnitzel as well. She is a real pearl, Katherine. A winner. She stays a week. One night, Tammie (aka Cupcakes, Scarlet) calls Henry at 2 a.m.; he invites her over; she leaves at 6 a.m. but is back two nights later at 4 a.m. She is high—probably does not know the correct time, or even the correct day. She is an empty-headed slut and pill-popper (Pamela O'Brien in 'real' life: "she's 23, brains, body, spirit…She'll be the death of me," Buk wrote. Pg. 214 LIVING ON LUCK, Letter to Carl Weissner). Henry loves her body but thinks her face cruel, and shark-like. A return, by Henry, to Joanne (6-footer) follows: She gives Henry mescaline; Henry, the old boozer, turns ugly on the trip and threatens to choke the woman…Henry takes Tammie with him to NYC. Tammie stays high all the time, and makes of herself a pain in Henry's ass. She nearly falls out the 10th story window of their hotel room. That's Tammie for you…Mercedes, a blue-eyed blonde, meets Henry at his reading and later jumps in the sack with him. Their sex is like a fight: Henry "rips" her, slaps her across the face, and calls her "whore."

Sex scenes of the novel are mostly without the satirical humor Henry Miller brought to his descriptions of the hydraulics of the acts. Buk's writing of sex in WOMEN lacks the aplomb of Miller's writing on the subject. Miller one of the few writers who could make comical the 'dirty deed.' Buk can't seem to pull his head out from between the legs of his women long enough to look around: his descriptions are obvious, repetitive, and ultimately boring.

Cecelia shows up on scene. Her husband, one of Chinaski's poet-buddies, has died suddenly. Henry demands sex from the grieving widow. She refuses. The refusal does not sit well with old Ubermensh Chinaski:

his ego, it seems, is threatened. His identity, newly adopted, as lady-killer, is in question due to Cecelia's denial. Henry becomes passive-aggressive. Cecelia flees…Welcome Liza, a ballerina and another class act…Another clichéd act of intercourse. Cassie, another blonde, likewise met at a Chinaski reading: she is twenty-something to Henry's 60. Another pill-popper too, and also on the coke. Henry passes on the coke, but takes an upper. He can't complete the job begun in bed (maybe it was a downer); it happens, says Cassie. Might not be the pill but the booze. Seems an inability to finish, plagues Henry regularly. But not while with Debra, an old fashioned girl who wears clothes reminding Henry of women of the 30's and 40's—like his mother perhaps…Nylons and garters, girdles, and high heels, long skirts…Sara, another groupie, is met at a reading also; she a little different than the others; a little more stable, mature—more on the ball: She owns a health food restaurant and is celibate; no sex outside marriage—in obedience to her guru, the Maharoni of Fungol. The celibacy thing is an affront to Henry. As Ubermensch he takes the abstinence as insult and challenge to his masculinity. He becomes irritable, out-of-sorts around Sara. Meanwhile, Iris flies into L. A. from Vancouver to see Henry. A belly dancing waitress. Her appearance complicates things for Henry. He manages. Sara soon becomes Henry's main squeeze—but there is a Tanya in the wings. Henry rationalizes his behavior by reminding himself that King Solomon had 700 wives. Tanya comes, and goes. Henry declares to Sara that she is number one with him. But he continues with pick-up's on streets and off of planes…In final pages Henry refuses a proposition—maybe for the first time ever…Seems he has begun to separate sex from love. Or has he? The refusal begins Henry thinking of himself as a moral being, even a "good" man, whereas previously referring to himself as "infantile" and "despicable drizzling shit." He has found a "good" woman in Sara, he thinks; a good woman for a good man—the new somewhat reformed Henry Chinaski!

Of the five Bukowski Chinaski novels WOMEN is my least favorite. The writing is flat—result of that "damaging lack of aesthetic distance" (pg. 123 Brewer). Flatter than Hemingway ever became (except maybe in ACROSS THE RIVER AND INTO THE TREES, 1950, and FOR WHOM THE BELL TOLLS, 1940, and GREEN HILLS OF AFRICA, 1935 and UNDER KILIMANJARO, 2005). Buk's humor saves the thing from being second rate: keeps it afloat. Like Hem, Buk could never write a wholly bad book. WOMEN is not a bad book, just not as good a book as other of Bukowski's Chinaski novels. One of the major problems of WOMEN being the women, all of whom, with exceptions (Lydia, Sara) are one dimensional characters, caricatures, manikins, and interchangeable, in bed and out. Buk himself had reservations about the novel, bemoaning in a letter to Carl Weissner (pg. 152, BUKOWSKI ON WRITING. Ed. Abel Delbritto) that though a good novel WOMEN would have been a greater one without John Martin interfering with the text; to Gerald Locklin (pg. 260 LIVING ONL LUCK) Buk wrote: "Martin went too far (on cuts) I guess he thinks I can't write." Martin's inexcusable re-writing and over-editing of Bukowski's work would show-up again in Black Sparrow's posthumously published Bukowski collections.

INTERNATIONAL BUK

Bukowski had become a big hit in Germany after his German translator, Weissner, helped see Bukowski's NOTES WRITTEN BEFORE JUMPING OUT an 8 STORY WINDOW into print. The book sold 50,000 copies in Germany (pg. 195 Miles). The first Bukowski book translated and published in Germany had been NOTES but relatively few copies sold. Three books of Bukowski's short stories followed 8 STORY WINDOW, in Germany.

The drunken bum was in the money. Not Big Money, but, for a poet/writer, good money. Buk was becoming a special somebody. Not wanting the serendipity to end, he began trying to control his alcohol consumption, tapering off whenever signs of serious health trouble began (overheated, blotchy skin, shortness of breath, etc.). An act of will power beyond the capacity of most active alcoholics. Buk had the toughness of a survivor's mentality. (He thanked his father for toughening him up via the childhood beatings—a faux gratitude and way for Buk to deal with the massive resentment against the old man.)

In '75 Bukowski opted out of considerations of a bourgeois life-style for a return to previous haunts in East Hollywood. His new apartment one block from a liquor store; a massage parlor was across the street (pg. 202 Miles). Pimps and prostitutes around the corner. Buk settled into the squalor of Carlton Way, east of the Hollywood Freeway (pg. 201 Miles), and began, again, writing of so-called low-life conditions—work written in common vernacular language recording small events of daily life and revealing, by the way, brutal facts of life and nature.

At 54 years old and with his reputation as writer growing, and as publications brought in money, Buk started to get more ass than a toilet seat: young nubile and willing girls showing up on his doorstep (though not Linda King, who had made a clean break from Hank after a 5 year long run.)

Hank's newest flame a 23-year old well-endowed pill-head; former Miss Pussycat Theater of 1973, working as cocktail waitress at the time of meeting Buk. In WOMEN she is "Tammie." In real life, Pamela O'Brien, aka 'Cupcakes.' Buk's pursuit of her seems a case of his thinking with the wrong head. I suppose a case could be made for his always using the wrong head to think with; another case for an adolescence extending far beyond his teenage years…After Cupcakes's near fall out of the 10th story hotel window she decamped to spend time with a dental student.

The sudden availability of women was a double-edged sword for Buk. The female druggies who latched onto him found him an easy touch. A sugar-daddy who could be used through sex; a little sex, or a lot, or only the promise of…Hank, the old boozer, reportedly began to sample some of the drugs brought around, particularly the cocaine (pg. 217 Miles).

In the meantime, the neighborhood about had become more dangerous, more violent: people being murdered with more regularity in the streets. Hank was ready to leave. He got his chance when a groupie named Linda Lee Beighle introduced herself to Hank after one of his readings. Linda, Hank soon realized, was of more substance than other of the flighty insubstantial wraiths he had been consorting with. A different type than the full-blown masochists who move with such rapidity through the pages of WOMEN.

Linda Lee had rejected her privileged east-coast upbringing and become a rebellious child and spiritual seeker, making her way to India before joining the counter-culture folks in California. She owned and operated a health-food restaurant in Redondo Beach. At the time of meeting Bukowski she was celibate—in accordance with stipulations of her guru. She and Hank set-up house together. She also somehow inveigled the old reprobate to give up hard liquor and beer for wine, and to stop eating red meat. Hank also began, under her tutelage, a regiment of vitamins…He soon lost 20-pounds, but began gulping the wine like a thirsty wino.

Linda Lee, petite with golden hair (pg. 320 Cherkovski) accompanied Hank on his European tour, 1977-78. Hank was treated royally in Germany, where he met with his German Uncle Heinrich. In France Hank appeared on television as one of the panelists of a prestigious literary discussion program, and succeeded in making an ass of himself by insulting the host and other guests. After walking off the set during programming—in a drunken stupor—he pulled his jackknife on the security guards. He was lucky not to have been beaten or worse. Who says the gods do not take care of drunks and fools? Linda Lee reportedly disarmed him and the guards gave the infamous Bukowski the bum's rush to the street. As a result of his boorishness his book sales in France skyrocketed. The French public evidently approved of what they may have perceived as Buk's puncturing pretense of the show's highfalutin literary elites and intellectuals. Buk's outlandishness was on par with the Punk performances of the time, put on by Johnny Rotten, Sid Vicious, Wendy O Williams, and others.

(Note: I know there were 2 separate European trips, first to Germany, then France: I have rolled them together here. WFB.)

PLAY THE PIANO DRUNK LIKE A PERCUSSION INSTRUMENT UNTIL THE FINGERS BEGIN TO BLEED, 1979.

Poems of this absurdly titled volume were originally published in a monthly magazine, SPARROW, issued by John Martin to showcase poets that Black Sparrow Press published (pg. 288 Sounes).

The book starts in a nostalgic vein with pieces for deceased Jane and then with lyrical poems spread over the pages, some of which do not work for me. Then come Liza-poems (Dee Dee of WOMEN) whom Bukowski hooked-up with on the rebound from Linda King. These poems are followed by Buk staples—some highly imaginative work—troublewith-women poems, racetrack-poems, boxing match-poems…One poem on new girlfriend Linda Lee, whom the book is dedicated to.

Gershwin might be coming in over Buk's radio as he wrote, or Scriabin, or Ives. Or maybe the 'Bee,' Beethoven. The eighty year old San Francisco landlady who introduced Buk to symphony music started him off with Beethoven's 5th—a story that Barry Miles tells, gleaned from Buk's early short story 'Hard Without Music' published 1948 in MATRIX. "Feeding symphonies to…my landladies wooden, man-high Victrola" (pg. 17, PORTIONS, Ed. D. S. Calonne). (But, if Buk's novel HAM ON RYE, 1982, is accurate regarding Buk's life, he was, like Chinaski, listening to classical music in his room at age 18, after having made acquaintance of the music in a downtown L. A. record store.)

In his poem 'classical music and me' Bukowski lists some favorites: Brahms, Tchaikovsky, Sibelius, Wagner, Haydn, Handel, Eric Coates, Bach, and Mahler. Classical music, he writes in a poem, "gave heart to my life." Buk liked many kinds of music—"anything that contains the original joy" he wrote in 'one for the shoeshine man.' But, as he told one interviewer, classical music is the "best" music (CD, BUKOWSKI, BORN INTO THIS, 2004, J. Dullaghan, Director). "I like all the German composers, plus a few Russians," Chinaski states in WOMEN. In a letter to Daniel Halpern (pg. 189 COLL. Letters, Vol. 4), Buk wrote "I have never written anything without the radio on to classical music." In a 1974 essay, "Dirty Old Man Confesses," Buk wrote that Mahler made both Beethoven and Bach "look like sissies" (pg. 193 PORTIONS).

I suspect that symphony music encouraged the Sturm und Drang found in Bukowski's poetry. Maybe as impetus in his creation of drama and emotionalism (Wagner) he interjected into his work? "More blood, more style" in classical music that in rock or jazz Buk wrote (pg. 46 COLL. Letters, Vol. 4. Letter to Luciano Capretti). One Bukowski commentator found 300 references to 50 different composers in Bukowski's writings.

THE LIFE STYLE OF THE BOURGEOISIE

On return to the United States from Europe Hank went completely bourgeois, shacking-up with Linda Lee in a big house in San Pedro, overlooking San Pedro Bay, at the southern end of the Los Angeles sprawl.

Hank was in Fat City. The house came with a $400 a month mortgage, but the price no problem as Hank's Black Sparrow honorarium had risen to $500 monthly and sales of his books on the European market were significant ("$100,000 yearly"—pg. 245 Miles).

Out in Hank's driveway sat a new BMW, bought off the car lot for $16,000. In the backyard a Jacuzzi and swimming pool. Fresh fruit could be had for the plucking, off fruit trees in the garden.

After 3 years together, and a 4th year on and off, Linda Lee and Hank decided to get married. As groom, Buk wore a new suit and snake skin shoes: none of his friends could recall ever seeing him dressed in a suit.

Thus Linda began her role, in earnest, as nursemaid, mommy to an erring boy, and wife of 64 year old Charles Bukowski. Linda was also, reportedly, a drinking partner of Hank's and if Bukowski's short story "Had Enough" applies to 'real' life, Linda, as 'Sara' in the story, could match her husband drink for drink.

Bukowski wrote the screenplay for a movie titled BARFLY, finishing the script in 1979-80 and being paid $10,000. The film to be directed by Barbet Schoroeder, an Iranian-born French citizen whose indefatigable efforts behind the scenes brought the movie to the big screen.

Barbet Schoroeder also filmed at the San Pedro house, capturing moments and scenes of the Bukowski's domestic life. One such recorded scene has become infamous, and led, erroneously, to Bukowski being labeled a "male chauvinist pig and wife-beater." As the camera is recording, Bukowski sits alongside his wife on a couch and is spewing venom until he savagely kicks her and she goes flying off the couch. Buk biographers Sounes and Miles both report that Bukowski, at the time of the incident, was in an alcoholic black-out and had no recollection, the morning after, as to what had transpired during the interview. Linda Lee claimed that nothing like it ever happened again, nor, that it—the physical violence—had ever happened previously.

With BARFLY, which was first titled THE RATS OF THIRST, Hank became a "real" celebrity. Other celebrities were curious to meet the poet of low-life bohemia. Sean Penn and his wife Madonna sought-out Hank in San Pedro. Bukowski liked Penn and the two formed a friendship; Hank did not like Madonna. Hank also met Norman Mailer, the sawed-off self-proclaimed heavyweight champ of the American literary world. Mailer, by his own account, stared Buk down after Buk suggested that he and Mailer might have to fight.

Hank received requests to appear on American television. One of the requests from producers of the TONIGHT SHOW starring Johnny Carson.

Johnny: (to Hank) So, when did you start to write poetry?

Hank: (smoking a beedie—Mangalore Ganesh Beedies, rolled by lepers) Well…Let's see now…I began to write…poetry…when I was around 35 years old…I had just come out of L. A. General Hospital…Around '54 or… '55 I think it was…

Johnny: You were in the hospital? Nothing too serious, I hope.

Hank: Well…I had been vomiting blood—great quantities…Waterfalls of blood, from my mouth, and my rectum.

Johnny: That can't be a good sign can it?

(Audience yuks it up)

Johnny: Listen, we have to take a break now. (Rapping pencil on desk top.) For a word from our sponsor. (He holds up a box of Preparation H, does a double-take looking at the box.) "Oh, no…!"

Ed McMahon: (roars) Ho ho ho ho ho.

Hank, perhaps recalling the French television fiasco (told the story by Linda Lee perhaps or had seen the tape) wisely turned the TONIGHT show and others (60 MINUTES) down.

During the 80's volumes of poetry and prose streamed from Bukowski's typer like the black turds he claimed came out his ass in '54 or '55.

WAR ALL THE TIME, 1982

This book opens with 'Horsemeat' a nearly 30-page saga of the horse race track. Something like the WAR & PEACE of horse racing. One would think, after reading 'Horsemeat' that Buk exhausted the subject but no, more race track-poems follow, most about the characters Buk encountered there, not the horses. Some unsavory character types among the crowd (it goes without saying that Buk is a character himself).

Buk's life in the 80's was limited compared to what transpired in earlier years. Not as limited as latter periods, described in up-coming volumes, but WAR and subsequent collections are represented heavily by nostalgic pieces recalling the old life rather than reporting on anything new. Nostalgia erupting in eulogizing poems of long dead Jane (Cooney Baker) whom Bukowski could not exorcise from his memory. Plus poems from Buk's days living at Carlton Way when his best friends were an owner of a porno store and the owner's girlfriend, a stripper. In an uncollected story "The Ladies Man of East Hollywood" (pg.221-45, CHARLES BUKOWSKI, The Absence of the Hero, Ed. D. S. Calonne) Bukowski describes in detail his acquaintanceship with the owner of the porno store, Todd, and Todd's stripper girlfriend. It is a story of the tawdry ugliness of Bukowski's life at the time. A time he, reportedly, began snorting coke as well as sucking down the booze. Photos taken of him at this time—by Linda King and Joan Gannij, and reproduced in Howard Sounes' Bukowski biography, picture a Buk with a definite Mephistophelian cast to his facial features.

Young girls, including Cupcakes, were using Buk's pad as a hang-out or rendezvous for certain illicit activities. 'overhead mirror,' 'girls from nowhere,' 'ass but not class,' and 'making it' all refer to Buk's life around 1975—almost ten years prior to his writing WAR.

Further nostalgia pieces concern Buk's poetry readings at college venues (which he gave up doing after his circumstances improved). Poems concerning his parents; concerning former working days (the Post Office and factories); childhood memories such as a piece about the L. A. Rams—the only poem I know of in which Buk uses NFL football as subject. All the familiar tropes are in existence: Linda Lee the "wife"; their 8 cats, Buk's desk and study room and staples of wine, beer, cigars, cigarettes; the neighbors, such as the 95 year old guy next door...and around the tropes, anything out of order, like some rudeness, ugliness, or even loveliness, like young girls skating with grace and aplomb ('the skaters') goes into the poetry which is Buk's most consistent staple of all (" 5,000 poems written over a span of fifty years"—intro., ESSENTIAL BUKOWSKI, Ed. Abel Debritto).

Buk now wrote using an IBM selectric typewriter. He drank expensive French and German wines. He could afford to: in 1984 he earned in excess of $110,000 from his writings (pg. 205 Sounes).

YOU GET SO ALONE AT TIMES THAT IT JUST MAKES SENSE, published in 1986, is a whopper of a collection (313 pgs.) The book written in Buk's San Pedro study. Written at night, early evening to early morning—while Linda Lee, downstairs, watching television maybe, or in bed.

The book starts with a poem of experience, 'red mercedes' then a good memory-poem on the habits and death of Buk's father, 'retired.'

The minimalist mature Bukowski style is found here: wonderfully succinct lines and poems written in high gloss clarity. A style I much prefer over the more lyrical poems and pieces of earlier works.

Buk drove a BMW now: the car started his series of freeway-poems—"the freeway...a circus of cheap and petty emotions" ('drive through hell'). Adventures of Buk on trips to and from the race track, along L. A. freeways. The amount of these poems not close to the number of racetrack-poems, but are a sub-sub-genre in the ocuvre.

The freeway, like the track, become metaphor for the condition of humankind at large (not good).

'in my first affair with that older woman' Bukowski lays bare his time spent with Jane, stressing his innocence, recognizing her mistreatment of him and the extent of his love for her. A sobering evaluation of himself, and possibly, the only woman he ever really loved (in his fashion). "The only real woman and real friend I could ever stand" (pg. 26 LIVING ON LUCK, Letter to J.W. Corrington). In another letter, this one to Patricia Connell (pg. 114 LIVING ON LUCK) Buk writes that he has been in love twice. I assume the 2nd woman is Linda King. A 3rd would be added later—Linda Lee.

A few poems of the old days in Philly, when Buk was a starving artist who became a starving drunk—the start of his putative 10-year non-writing lay-off, a claim integral to the Bukowski mythos—his rising like a phoenix—like an Ubermensch, from the ash can of life to fame and fortune.

A self-congratulatory tone to some pieces: for his, the poet's survival and endurance. And some wonder too over how he survived; why things worked-out for him as they had…In between the congratulation, gratitude, and wonder, are visits into the past: to a Tijuana whorehouse; L. A. High School, Mount Vernon Junior High, Grammar School; poems of life with Jane (drunk, drinking); a poem about a stripper the poet admired back in 1935…Short blurbs, or blurts, of discontent, as in 'shoes' and 'true.' Reminiscence of time in hospital, and in Miami where the poet, broke, lived on one candy bar a day.

David Stephen Calonne, in his Buk study CHARLES BUKOWSKI, wrote that in these poems "theme, form, and style are deftly fused."

THE BIG TIME

In 1982 Hank published his 37th book, a novel.

Returning to earliest memories to recreate his nightmare childhood and adolescence, but without bathos. A bildungsroman titled HAM ON RYE, which could aptly be sub-titled 'The Education of Henry Chinaski, The Early Years.'

Young Henry's mother calls her husband, Henry's father, "Daddy." He calls her "Mama." Both are emotionally stunted human beings in no way equipped to raise a child.

Henry is an inquisitive boy—unfortunately he addresses his questions to his father. The father is a Prussian and a nut-case as well as cruel racist prick. He is also the funniest and most interesting character of the story.

Young Henry goes off to school: the School of Early Constipation. Henry is hung-up on his bodily functions and saves his number-2 until he returns home from school. But sometimes, even after he returns home, he loses the urge to go. It is a bad sign for the boy's future: the feces hardens within him; he hardens too, on his way to the Frozen man syndrome; that is, emotionally withdrawn and unable to feel intensely about anything.

Henry attracts other loners and outcasts of the school to him. Like "David" who wears knickers and is regaled as a "sissy" by the other boys—who bully David unmercifully (but for whatever reason, not Henry).

Henry's father, Henry Senior, becomes a lot less funny when he starts beating young Henry with a razor strop. After the first, of many beatings, Henry asks his mother why she did not stop the father's abuse.

She answers: "The father is always right." Her implicit acquiescence in the beatings seals Henry's doom. He comes to feel utterly alone and forsaken (the mother soon gets in line for her beatings).

Meanwhile, the boy indulges himself in a fantasy world, day-dreaming that he is a baseball player hitting over .500 as well as a great football quarterback. The fantasies get him into trouble. Walking with head in the clouds, Henry gets run down by an automobile—but is not seriously hurt.

He picks up most of his education in the schoolyard from other kids. One student tells Henry how "it" is done (with the appropriate pantomime). Henry files the information, his ideas about life and existence rapidly changing. Sex has entered the equation of life's mathematics.

Henry is in the 6th grade: it is the worse year of the Great Depression in America. Men without jobs, some without hope. They are angry men, and their kids are angry too—even the animals seem angry. Everyone, man, woman, and child of the neighborhood is tough. Tough times produce tough people. Tough angry people.

Like William Saroyan, James T. Farrell, and John Steinbeck, Bukowski also is a depression-era writer, and carried the stoicism and toughness of a survivor with him through life.

In Junior High School, while hanging around with a kid named 'Baldy,' Henry is introduced to alcohol. It is magical: upon taking a few drinks of Baldy's father's wine, the world instantly looks better to Henry—more alive somehow, like him.

Then comes the acne: like one of the plagues of Egypt, Henry is visited by one of the worst cases of "acne vulgaris" the doctors at L. A. General Hospital have seen. Description of the treatment and Henry's feelings around his disfigurement is memorably done; but then, so is the rest of the book.

In the public library Henry discovers another new world—like the worlds of sex and alcohol, the world of literature opens Henry's eyes to new possibilities. He wallows in the writings of Upton Sinclair, Sinclair Lewis, D. H. Lawrence, H.D., Aldous Huxley, Sherwood Anderson, and Ernest Hemingway—later adding Turgenev and Gorky to the list.

Meanwhile, the old world continues for Henry as it always has: he remains an outsider in High School, as in grade school. L. A. High School, which his father insisted Henry attend—instead of more conveniently located though less renown schools nearer the family's home.

Henry takes R.O.T.C. with other misfits of the school, instead of gym class, because in gym he would be obligated to remove his shirt and thus reveal the boils covering his torso.

Much of life seems absurd to our reluctant hero, who, like other adolescent characters—such as Holden Caulfield and Hamlet, is troubled by his perception of a world of falsity, and whose honest doubt leads him to incessant questioning of the nature of so-called 'reality.' (Bukowski praised CATCHER IN THE RYE, 1951, J. D. Salinger's novel. "HAM ON RYE" could be seen as a play on Salinger's title. Buk had nothing good to say about the Bard of Avon.)

Henry graduates and then goes to work as stock-boy for 'Mears-Starbucks,' just as young Hank went to work at Sears & Roebucks—and as Henry Chinaski worked at any number of menial jobs in FACTOTUM and elsewhere.

…It is 1940, and Henry is enrolled as a student of journalism at L. A. City College—after being fired from his stock-boy gig. Far from the confines of sweet college life—across an ocean—in Henry's country of origin, Adolf Hitler and his Nazis are putting people into concentration camps and the Gestapo is taking others into the basement of Prince-Albrechtstress 8 in Berlin for a chat, and more. Out of contrariness Henry suddenly discovers a residual patriotism for the old Fatherland.

He joins campus right-wingers of the fascist American Party—just before he goose-steps out of college…

Post-college, Henry enters a macho-phase. The number of guys he beats up and/or throws down the stairs of his rooming house strains verisimilitude, but, who cares? The Ubermensch has arisen and is kicking ass and taking down names. Fighting and drinking, drinking and fighting. No women yet though: Henry is chastely macho. Two who did offer—Henry's buddy's mother, and a college professor, were turned down by Henry who seems an oddly bashful Ubermensch.

Leaving his rooming house, Henry settles into another, this one on Bunker Hill where one of Bukowski's literary heroes, John Fante, once lived: where the great Arturo Bandini was born and struggled with the word and found acceptance by the even greater H. L. Mencken. Bandini/Chinaski: They are almost interchangeable, Bandini only a mensh however, while Chinaski, the real deal Ubermensch. (In his short story "I Meet the Master," pg. 205-30 PORTIONS, Buk has Chinaski, who has memorized descriptions of the neighborhood, seek out the location of the building where Fante lived while writing ASK THE DUST and then knocking on the door of the room Fante occupied—to be confronted by an angry woman who slams the door in Henry's face.)

The Day of Infamy arrives: December 7, 1941. Dastardly Pearl Harbor Day. Henry decides not to enlist in the Armed Services. Not interested in being a patriot or in fighting for any cause except his own.

Buk's descriptions of his protagonist's young manhood verge toward the cartoonish, but the childhood re-telling and adolescent saga seems to me the deepest Buk ever ventured in that realm. Far deeper than in any other of his novels. Critics such as Gay Brewer and Howard Sounes write of the somberness of the story but fail to mention the humor of the thing—particularly in Buk's portrayal of the whack-job father. Also funny is the comedic dead-pan tone used throughout: the sangfroid of a narrator who keeps his objectivity while describing the most horrific events.

Buk began work on another novel, HOLLYWOOD, in 1988, drawing his material from those he had met during filming of the movie BARFLY. Also, in '88, Black Sparrow Press put out another Buk poetry volume, THE ROOMING HOUSE MADRIGALS.

What is a madrigal? A madrigal is a part-song for several voices arranged in elaborate counterpoint (Google).

The book starts out like something written or dictated by Hemingway. There is a bull, maybe two bulls, a senorita, maybe more than one, and a battle taking place somewhere—where, is unclear; things are amorphous, vague…Comes a poem on one of Buk's pet peeves: other poets—those mostly effete, according to Buk, others. The coddled and soft ones who never had to work laboring, never starving to death while living in a shack (like Buk in Atlanta), never going to jail: those supported by mother or some other woman, or by a University. Those glory hunters, exhibitionists…"Slime who do it out of vanity and ego" (pg. 40 COLL. Letters, vol. 4. Letter to W. Packard). Those "who want to get published for the sake of getting published" (pg. 43 COLL. Letters, vol. 4. Letter to J. Martin). There are a few good ones, Buk admits. Among the good, Wantling, Blazeck, Webb, Norse, Richmond; plus a few good old ones: Li Po, Robinson Jeffers, Catullus. The goodness of the rest questionable (see 'see here, you!').

These are big poems, bouncing all over the place, line to line even, stanza to stanza, in contrapuntal fashion (that "elaborate counterpoint"). Blustery poems too; some flippancy; a few poems uncharacteristically cute—some glistening in their own sweat, so hard had they to work just getting onto the page: a couple of weird ones, like over-extended metaphors that surpass comprehension (mine). The great 'The Genius of the Crowd' is, surprisingly, among this early work.

The poems slowly come into focus and achieve more clarity. Less slippery of meaning. Less blustery, less flighty; not as much counterpoint, but so what? The romance diminutives of 'oh' and 'ah' and 'o' used early in the book fade and the evanescent assumes more body, less air…Finally.

A couple dozen ending pages of powerful work saves the book from mediocrity. The pretense plus faux-Hemingway drivel are not enough, for me, despite some startling imagery throughout.

A difficult book to like but interesting as document charting Sir Charles' evolution as poet. He did not arrive, you learn, from the god's head full-blown. The early prose (40's) suffers the same defect of the early poetry—being self-consciously over-literary. According to Jules Smith (pg. 116 ART, SURVIVAL, AND SO FORTH) the poems in MADRIGAL were revived from early Buk magazine publications but significantly altered by changes in language and syntax in book publication: "slang and swear words" omitted, and "speech regularized."

THE HOME STRETCH

Sometime in 1989 Hank ran a fever of 103.0 while feeling himself in a run-down condition. Multiple trips to prominent Beverly Hills doctors were of little use; none able to explain Hank's low hemoglobin count, lethargy, and general malaise. It was a veterinarian, whom Bukowski had brought his cat to, who suggested possibility of tuberculosis, a suggestion that an X-ray confirmed (none of the Beverly Hills docs had ever seen a TB case among their well-to-do patients). In four months Bukowski's weight dropped from 217 lbs. to 175 (pg. 89 COLL. Letters, vol. 4. Letter to W. Packard). The course of antibiotics prescribed, plus a withdrawal from alcohol (alcohol verboten) froze Hank's brain so solidly that for a period he could no longer write creatively. Since the disease is contagious, Buk was isolated in a sick-room and bed where he slept upright on two pillows. During the day he, reportedly (pg. 42 COLL. Letters, vol. 4. Letter to W. Packard), watched television, which he disliked; out of boredom, he watched the L. A. Dodger's baseball games—though he thought baseball "like a slow chess match moving toward death" ('1970 blues').

Buk's hard-drinking days were nearly over. When pronounced cured in November of '89—his weight down to 155 lbs. (pg. 42 COLL. Letters, vol. 4. Letter to W. Packard)—he began again to nip, but on beer and wine only. His non-drinking period had been "the longest almost 6 months" of his life, he wrote ('the gigantic thirst').

HOLLYWOOD

This novel a roman a clef, meaning some of the characters are famous or well-known people, slightly disguised. A critic for the Toronto Star newspaper called the book "good" and called the movie BARFLY, which is the subject of the novel, "mediocre." The critic was seconded, about book and movie, by a host of others, though the movie had a respectable run in theaters. The book continues to sell, as of this writing, 2023.

Sarah, "the wife" of the story (Linda Lee) is one of the most amusing and interesting characters of the novel. Her comments and asides give a dose of sanity to what, by any measure, are "crazy" proceedings.

When Sarah disappears from the narrative, she leaves primarily Henry and Jon Pinchot (Barbet Schroeder) the director, center stage, among a cast of producers, executives, and other businessmen crooks (along with a few prima-donna actors). Jon is a lively character, and so is Henry, always; but the book stalls a bit around mid-point before regrouping for a strong finish.

Drama of the story is sustained by the effort of the participants to bring the BARFLY script, and story, to the big screen. Also, by what goes on on-set. The hijinks of film-making—as Chinaski views it.

Without the film, we'd have another Chinaski story of racetrack, wirting, drinking, and more drinking (including another Chinaski screed against "reformed alcoholics," as he says, whom he erroneously believes to be Bible-thumping religionists under deep psychological stress of abstinence). A Henry-story, but with Sarah too, and Sarah is good for the novel as foil to Chinaski. She completes him somehow in their coupling. Like Gracie with George, Lucy with Desi, Alice with Ralph;

her jokiness and level-headedness compliment Henry's comedy act, adding some needed pizazz to it.

As to the movie, Bukowski had a few criticisms—made to Teresa Leo (pg. 171, COLL. Letters, vol. 4). Fay Dunaway, who played the "Jane" character, did not play Jane "insane enough." Mickey Rourke's clothing style was wrong: the real barfly, Hank, always wore clean clothes. Also, the barroom fight scenes were too "brutal," not reflecting truly the reality of Buk's drunken brawls.

The racetrack keeps Henry, and Hank, in touch with the reality of what humankind consists of—which is not much, Henry/Hank opines. A brutal and sometimes sad reality—like much of Henry's/Hank's former life.

Bukowski needed the racetrack but admitted that going to the track was a "sickness." A "need" any gambler would instantly understand. The need for action. The need to escape aforesaid 'brutal' realities. Escape via the thrill of the race. Every addict can play the tune: the rooms of AA, NA, OA, and GA are full of them. And so are the cemeteries.

Of course, drinking is an escape too, an escape from reality. A necessary escape for a self-proclaimed "coward" like Bukowski claimed to be. He thanks the gods for the efficacy of alcohol, and the track, in enabling him to break free occasionally of the onerous constraints of reality, so-called. I would venture to say, as well, that escape from reality kept Buk from any serious in-depth analysis of his own character, and that alcohol and gambling, though serving as escape routes, became, finally, inescapable as well. The personal freedom he sought for himself was not possible to obtain due to his addictions. He was not, in any case, someone to whom 'self-improvement' was desirable. He dismissed remorse and guilt in the aftermath of his less memorable performances—refused to go there—and seems ('seems' because who knows what he thought privately, in innermost self) to have accepted himself as a flawed character. This sense of self-acceptance comes through in his late poems particularly, in which he seems, remarkably so, at peace with himself, and "disporting," as Melville said, in "mute calm" from a fevered center. (But, again, whether he was or wasn't truly at peace with himself remains impossible to know.)

I here take leave of HOLLYWOOD, an entertaining and breezily-told story—a work as funny as A CONFEDERATE GENERAL IN BIG SUR, Richard Brautigan's outrageously comical 1964 novel. I and we also take leave of Henry Chinaski, as HOLLYWOOD is Chinaski's last starring novelistic role.

I now intend to deal, through summation and exegesis, with two of Bukowski's greatest collections.

DANGLING IN THE TOURNEFORTIA, 1981, is one of Buk's strongest works— of tightly wrapped poems in a mix of jokiness and seriousness.

Prose-y poems about the 1930's in America and about Buk's relationship with Linda ('Lydia' of WOMEN). Written transcripts of Linda's talk/screech taking poor Buk to task while he hung-over, slumped in a chair, and drinking, drinking…Poems detailing the end of a folie de deux of a relationship between two narcissists. Each trying to step out of their self-love to include the other, and each repeatedly failing. The inevitable ending brings realization to her of never being made to laugh again by his jokes; and to him the fact of never seeing her again in all her "sleeping beauty."

Poems about the women of WOMEN speak deeper truths than ever came to the surface of that novel. This work a sort of addendum to WOMEN. The same familiar faces, and feces: fights, reconciliations, breakup's and break-down's…

The book includes some classic Buk poems: 'on the hustle' and 'the secret of my endurance' among others. Reflections on his past poetry readings on college campuses. Buk qualified himself as a Dirty

Old Man in a poem in which he describes himself getting an erection while holding his girlfriend's young daughter. He also continues, according to the poetry, to masturbate, even when he has a steady girlfriend. Is pleasuring himself a means of reducing his anxiety? Or auto-erotic feature of his self-love? Or is it self-hate? Let's call Doctor Stekel and the good doctor Freud. Let's put into evidence a letter Buk wrote to William Wantling in 1966 (pg. 223 SCREAMS), wherein Buk states that he would rape little girls if not for "social consciousness" and "the chance of getting caught." Let's call in Doctors Jung and Phil. Buk compounds the offending remark to Wantling by stating, in amelioration, that the victims, the innocents, have "died or slipped or slurred or murdered something themselves"—even the small girls. Let's call in Rank, Ellis, and Doctor Ruth. Hell, I will speak to them as well…Buk does blame, in a following letter to Wantling, such louche comments on his boozing.

DANGLING written at the time of Buk's move to San Pedro—to suburbia. Coming down from the hustle of East Hollywood and still somewhat healthy, physically, in his late 50's.

Comfortable nights with the missus; days lying under the fruit trees with his cats. There is a balcony attached to his upstairs study and the plumbing in the house is copper, but he is still doing his work, he reflects, as he always has—in a small room.

Admirers show-up at his door, some he lets in. Many have come to praise his "genius." To Buk, the genius label is a joke, and so is much of the rest: fame, money, celebrity—a cosmic joke of gods who, unexplainably, have plucked him off a barstool and set him down on a small golden throne.

SEPTUAGENARIAN STEW, 1990, is called "great" by Howard Sounes. The book published in Bukowski's 70th year.

Buk had begun writing using a Macintosh computer that his daughter, an engineer, had installed for him. And wife had paid for. Buk took to the thing like a duck to water, and doubled his usual large output of work. Some of the stuff bad, not up to former standards. The "bad" stuff—'bad' a relative term here, ended up in Buk's posthumously published collections. Work heavily, and unfortunately, edited, by John Martin who managed, too often, to make Buk sound like Rod McKuen.

The STEW is classic Bukowski. A run of autobiographical-seeming poems are followed by the short stories "Son of Satan," and "The Life of a Bum," two great ones. "Satan" may be, along with "Bring Me Your Love," the best of Bukowski's many tales. "The Life of a Bum" is much quieter than the other two mentioned stories, but great also.

A slew of race track poems, of varying success, follows the stories. The track and it's people: the few winners, many losers; the jockeys, horse-owners, concession venders, valets, bartenders, ticket-takers, whores, and the hoi polloi in states of hope, desperation, and delirium…Bukowski is the A. J. Liebling of the race track crowd. The poetry contains a sociological dimension as well: of the rich & poor, white and non-Anglo races, young and old, all viewed by our narrator, commonly referred to as "Hank," from his seat in the grandstand, though, as in his story "The Jockey's" Hank is invited occasionally , on the strength of his reputation as a writer, into the clubhouse and afterward to the stable (by '83 Buk got Turf Club parking and passes to the turf club and box seats at Santa Anita and Los Alamitos tracks.)

In 'cleaning the ranks,' a defensive screed of a poem, Buk affirms Ubermensch status through another attack on "reformed alcoholics." Traitors, he calls them, to the tribe of Ubermensch drunks, such as the great Bulouski, who claims to have drunk more of booze than any reformer has drunk of water. Way to go, Buk!

Elsewhere in his work, Buk calls himself "alcoholic"—at least as many times as he denies being one. Such a defensive posture, as in the poem mentioned above, is constructed out of fear: fear someone will take his booze away. A catastrophic threat to someone, like Buk, who believed booze a necessary adjunct for the creative act of writing. And writing, and being a published-writer, was a big part, the greatest part it could be fairly said, of Bukowski's self-identity. Yet, during periods of enforced abstinence, or the few times he willingly became "dry," he continued to write, and write well. So his defensiveness when confronted by the sobriety of the reformed crowd is, obviously, a cover for some deep underlying personal issues that Buk did not care to address; he used denial instead of doing the laborious and sometimes onerous work of self-examination some of those "reformed alcoholics" did in addressing "issues."

In his poem 'The Rape of the Holy Motha' Bukowski issues a manifesto, or broadside, of sorts, to those poets he deems 'Academic.' Those who prefer their poetry secretive, soft, and nearly or wholly indecipherable. The fakers and frauds, soft babies, who will be pushed aside Buk posits, by the new poets from bars, jails, and back-alleys; those who will rally to the cause of replacing the mostly dead and mostly white entrenched snobs of the academies, who are but the latest vanguard of what Bukowski considers the swindle of the passing-on of a mostly lifeless literature as the REAL thing. A scandal perpetrated by the cognoscenti to continue as power-brokers and self-proclaimed authorities. A century's long fraud…

The indie and little poets, led by Chief Buk, have flung down the gauntlet and Rome is beginning to fall…Let's hope it finally topples.

In his poem 'just trying to get a little service' Buk stands-up for the geriatric crowd when he faces-off with two rude punks in a restaurant, inviting them to "step outside" and duke it out. An invite they turn down: they're punks, and their gutlessness remains intact.

The baseball stories in the 2nd half of this 375 page book, are unlike any that Ring Lardner wrote—unlike any anyone else ever wrote I suspect, and a welcome addition to the poetry.

I will second Barry Miles' opinion of the volume: "on target, no tricks, just honed skill."

SHORT STORIES.

SOUTH OF NO NORTH, 1973, includes a mildly amusing fantasy of Chinaski beating hell out of Hemingway in a boxing match. The fingerprints and spirit of Hem are all over this uneven collection.

In the story "Remember Pearl Harbor" Chinaski has it made in jail as big winner at craps in the jail yard. Winning as frequently as he does at the racetrack, in other stories. Sometimes it seems as if Chinaski (Bukowski) cannot lose even if he wanted to. This is an element of the Ubermensch mythos. It would be bad form, and highly unlikely, for the Ubermensch to lose at anything. To lose would be comparable to his being beaten up by a sissified fellow. It would not happen: The myth of the Ubermensch—his indomitable heroism—is predicated upon his winning. The mighty Thor never lost at Parcheesi and neither does Chinaski. Bukowski has had a few, minor, set-backs, but never Chinaski, Ubermensch par excellence.

In the story "Politics" Chinaski hints that liquor the cause of his college infatuation with fascism. An exculpatory and not very convincing excuse for actions from the louche youth of Bukowski. In his poem 'what will the neighbors think' Buk states his pro-fascist letters to newspapers sent as provocation only—and were not meant to be taken seriously.

Like the sketches Hemingway wrote early in his career, so too do many of the tales here appear sketchy—episodes rather than developed short stories.

"Maja Thurrp" and a story about tiny human beings, "No Way to Paradise," do not work for me as satire. "Bop Bop Against the Curtain," and "Politics" are memoir fragments. Good, more developed stories are "The Killers," "Pittsburgh Phil & Co.," and "Something About a

Viet Cong Flag." In "A Shipping Clerk With a Red Nose" Buk as 'Randall Harris' is introduced by Bukowski doppelganger Chinaski. It is a clever story, but fairly uninteresting. "This is What Killed Dylan Thomas" another snap-shot memoir fragment. "No Neck and Bad As Hell" something like a slice from WOMEN, with Liza as 'Vicky.' The story takes an exceedingly odd turn when Hemingway shows up and chats with Chinaski. Why so much Hem anyway? To bolster the machismo of Chinaski's Ubermensch act? In his troubled and varied life Hemingway was poster-boy for the macho-crowd. He liked to play God as well—which is a step above Ubermensch. (As macho-man, and a killer of animals, by the score, Hem, when asked if he felt bad about all the killing, said no because he was only assuming prerogative of God, and thus—in a twisted piece of logic, in a twisted human being, killing was a 'spiritual' activity. THE MAN WHO WAS NOT THERE, title of Richard Bradford's 2018 Hemingway biography, killed NOT to feel closer to a god, or God, but to feel as a god, or God. They are going to die anyway (the animals) he also said…Bukowski was not known to kill anything but flies. In a letter to J. W. Carrington Buk comments "guess guys like Hem would think me queer"—pg. 20 LIVING ON LUCK.)

The story "The Way the Dead Love" has a touch of Dostoevsky's novel NOTES FROM THE UNDERGROUND, 1864, a work Buk claimed as an influence, along with Dos's novel CRIME AND PUNISHMENT, 1866. In "Confessions of a Man Insane Enough to Live With Beasts," Chinaski does half a shift in a slaughterhouse before walking off the job; he then runs into 'Vicky' (Jane) who becomes Henry's shack-job. They drink, fight, and love in their manner: an old story told with much greater effect in FACTOTUM.

The stories of HOT WATER MUSIC, 1983, are on par with Buk's stories in SEPTAGENARIAN STEW: much deeper than the stories of SOUTH OF NO NORTH and far less fragmented.

The doppelganger theme is replayed in "The Great Poet": a poet named Strachman, who lives in the YMCA and is crippled and helpless, is visited by an unnamed interviewer. The poet sounds much like Bukowski, sharing Buk's prejudices and obsessions. It is possible the interviewer is Chinaski.

A lot of farts are cut in these stories, most of them by the female characters. How many, you ask? I have not counted. More than enough for me. Many more than ever occurred in Henry James's collected works, certainly.

HOT LADY, which features the lady, the skeleton, the drink, and the Monk, is nothing like "The Gambler, the Nun, and the Radio" (Hem). In a bar, Monk confronts the past, all the way back to Joan of Arc. The Lady, named "Mud" and the skeleton, who serves drinks, add a surreal touch; the surreal something of an adventure in Buk's usually reality-based work, and one that reemerges in his final novel PULP.

Murderous and raw slices of life: whores and killers, bums and misbegotten, all crowded into the brutal city. "It's A Dirty World" is a story title. The rapist of another story is invited by his victim to her apartment but he cannot perform there—he's a rapist not a lover. A wife shoots her husband while he sleeps; when he wakes he shoots her; she reloads the gun and again shoots him. Cops show up to investigate: one cop says to the other that he hates domestic quarrels, because "too messy."

Critic Gay Brewer perceptively notes that the stories in HOT WATER predominantly feature the kitchen and not, as in SOUTH OF NO NORTH, the bedroom. The difference, along with the many stories featuring couples, signals that domesticity the main subject of HOT WATER, the action fluctuating "between poles of domestic security and inflated danger" (pg. 72 Brewer).

In one story a man casually slits the throat of another man. The killer returns home, eats a sandwich, and only remembers the murder after finding in his pocket the book of matches he took off the dead man. In another story a woman bites off part of the head of a man's penis. (Never, in any of the stories by Henry James that I have read (3) has such a thing happened. And speaking of James, Buk called his work "a light mist of silk"—pg. 48 SCREAMS. Letter to Ann Bauman).

UNCOLLECTED STORIES

In his story "The Reason Behind the Reason," 1946, Bukowski first introduces readers to Chelaski, later to become Chinaski, as a baseball player who refuses to leave home plate after hitting the ball to the outfield for a hit. Chelaski stands at home while the fans go berserk and begin throwing things at him. Why he refuses to run is unclear. Why does Bartleby the Scrivener, in Melville's short story "Bartleby" say "I prefer not to" upon every request? Who knows? Buk's story may have been inspired by the Jimmy Piersall Story, book or movie. Piersall was a major league baseball player, for the Boston Red Sox and other teams, who in 1952 had a mental breakdown and had been institutionalized. The story could also or additionally be read as comment on alienation and the condition of the "Frozen Man."

Buk often took articles he read in the newspapers and used them as basis for stories. One such article was impetus for his story "Christ With Barbeque Sauce," 1970. Three cannibals, two male one female, drive around picking up hitch hikers and befriending them before killing and eating them. A delightful story.

A story more disgusting, if you can believe it, than the above, is "Absence of the Hero," 1969, a fecal-feast with other bodily wastes included. In its putridity the story is a not so subtle condemnation of humankind. Though I have never believed Bukowski's claim that he hated people—those "disgusting/spiritually destroyed/useless/babbling/ugly/fawning/humans" ('people'), this tale leads me to believe in his basic misanthropy.

The joy and despair of Buk's relationship with Jane is well-illustrated in "Sound and Passion," 1971, a sad and lonely tale that tells, more powerfully than any poem on the subject, of the relationship.

Another tale worth mention is "The Gambler," 1989, a story about the addicts' compulsion. If you think you are having a bad day, read about Shultz's buddy's day in Las Vegas—your day might improve or, at least, not seem so bad.

END GAME

By '92 Buk was receiving $7000 monthly from Black Sparrow Press and Martin, who had 17 of Bukowski's books in print—each selling at least 10,000 copies a year (pg. 231 Sounes).

LAST NIGHT OF THE EARTH POEMS, 1992, is the last of Buk's computer generated collections of poems published in his life-time. It is also the longest work, at 405 pages, that Black Sparrow published of Bukowski's work—until the 408 page posthumous volume WHAT MATTERS IS HOW WELL YOU WALK THROUGH THE FIRE, 1999. (CITY LIGHTS BOOKS did publish a longer work, ERECTIONS, EJACULATIONS.)

The poems of LAST NIGHT are compulsively readable. A handful of freeway-poems right at the checkered flag. Buk racing to win a senseless race against another speeder, and driving 18 miles past his destination to come out top-dog (sometimes you need to win SOMETHING).

Poems written in the aftermath of Buk's TB diagnosis and treatment. Six months of antibiotics made writing or even thinking straight difficult for Buk—but he had soldiered on. Rising from the canvas after receiving an 8-count.

The action is limited due to changed circumstances of his life: gone is the booze, bars, and broads. Hell, all that is left Buk for excitement is the racetrack, hence a slew of racetrack-poems, and, consequently, more freeway-poems. Other poems luxuriate in the quiet sanctity of the moment; poems that make the smallest parts of daily life larger; a love poem to Linda Lee (the wife); poems on the sorry state of modern poetry and poets: great poems such as 'bluebird,' 'we ain't got no money, honey, but we got rain,' 'Dinosauria, we,' and 'torched-out.' Poignant pieces about the closeness of Buk's approaching death, and his being ill and tired; kind of summation-poems of Buk taking stock, tallying up the years...

One poem describes a dream Bukowski has; him being able to fly, and those on the ground below reaching to pull him down, but unable to. The people below think that flying is easy, nothing to it; but Buk knows better (in the dream) knows that flying has to be worked-up to, that a lot of hard work is involved...The dream a metaphor illustrative of Buk's success; his rising above other poets and circumstances, and acknowledgement that such success did not come easy, no matter what anyone, like those on the ground, thought.

Diagnosed with leukemia in '93, Buk spent 64 days in the hospital receiving chemotherapy and antibiotics before returning home to San Pedro. According to doctors, his cancer had gone into remission. At Linda Lee's urging, Buk took-up TM, transcendental meditation (pg. 237 Sounes), part of what Buk, in a letter, called the "Aryuvedic Method." According to Linda Lee, Buk took TM classes and meditated twice daily, each session 20 minutes long (YOU TUBE video, interview of Linda Lee Bukowski).

The cancer returned. Doctors gave Buk one year to live, at best. He lasted eight months, 8-'93 to 3-'94, dying, age 73, on 3-9-94. His funeral was conducted as a Buddhist ceremony—through Linda's urging Buk had started giving consideration to Buddhist dharma in his last days.

Buk went to the Bardo to await return.

PULP, posthumously published in 1994, is Bukowski's last published novel. He had begun the book in '91 and was three-quarters done by '93 but became sick and was only able to return to writing the book after his cancer remission in 1993.

To have made his protagonist anti-hero a dick—a super-dick— how appropriate to Buk's Ubermensch image. The private eye, named

Belane (in memory of Mickey Spillane) is more or less Chinaski, only Chinaski with a license to beat or kill plenty of the 'apes' he meets in his line of work.

Bukowski's obsessions are on display here: death (there is a "Lady Death") and the scrotum. Sounds like a D. H. Lawrence title: Death and the Scrotum. Belane's scrotum mostly, but that of others as well. More references to 'balls' in the novel that in a broadcast of a pro-bowlers' tournament.

The fear of losing one's balls constitutes the greatest threat to Chinaski/Bukowski. The fear evident in the many references to castration in Buk's writings. See the short story "Praying Mantis," and the story "No Way to Paradise"; the poems 'true story,' and 'freedom.' The complex, or hang-up, seeming to do with Buk's sexual jealousy, a feature of all his relationships. (He was also hung-up on the size of his hands—believing them too small. A hang-up shared with novelist Malcolm Lowry, another angst-ridden and neurotic artist.)

Lady Death hangs around Belane. When he asks her why, she answers that she hangs around everyone, and Belane just happens to be more aware of her than others are. Belane cannot escape her: no one can. In the end she gets her man.

Chinaski-like, Belane is something of a nihilist with a dark sense of humor. His existentialist philosophy—cutting out God and possibilities of transcendence, takes the strength of a superman Ubermensch to adhere to. Following the Sartean line: no hope but no despair either. Like characters in a Sartre play, Belane/Chinaski are trapped in an unfair game, knowing that any notion of victory is absurd. Understanding the Sartean view of suicide as a valid and understandable response to the conundrum of existence, but neither opting for it…An existential "ethos," wrote Jules Smith, but "stripped of its theoretical and intellectual ramifications"—as found in the writings of Sartre and Camus (pg.112 Smith).

(Bukowski thought Hemingway's suicide an act of bravado, instead of, more accurately, an act of a mentally-ill person. Where, we might ask, does bravado end and insanity begin? In a bi-polar dance macabre like Hemingway stepped to? Like a maddened King Lear—exposing himself needlessly to gun-fire during WW II while working as correspondent—Hemingway was unable to separate reality from his fiction, and both turned into a vast confusion in his mind. He became unable to distinguish between fantasies of himself and reality of his actions. A kind of disassociated state became his norm and led, first, to the collapse of his writing, then his psyche.)

PULP contains some witty lines: "If we had talking livers we wouldn't need AA." "Definition of a nice neighborhood: a place you couldn't afford to live."

The work, as a whole, a little too cute for its own good, but with some fine surrealistic touches. The thing works as a comedy-caper, but is certainly Bukowski-light, and less-filling.

POSTHUMOUSLY

BETTING ON THE MUSE, 1996, is the first of the Bukowski posthumous collections Black Sparrow offered. Poems & stories still with the magic of the old Bukowski tomes. The work is, reportedly, a companion volume to Buk's SEPTUGENERIAN STEW.

Acerbic, inventive language cut to the bone. Powerful stories interspersed with the poetry. Less racetrack poems than usual. A couple of freeway shots. Buk swaggers through this collection, at the top of his game. A dozen or so poems about writing poems; poems about being a writer; and poems about other poets.

This is the kind of book you build a shrine around and bow down to 9 times daily. The equal, certainly, of the STEW.

A trio of John Fante-poems: Fante's essential greatness; Fante remembered.

Some tender and beautiful poems, such as 'let it enfold you' and 'the laughing heart,' that bathe in the present moment and convey the poet's final acceptance of life on life's terms, and the belief that the end of life is not a defeat but a victory of sorts; and that life, as harsh as it is, or can be, is also, or can be, sweet.

Poems as barometer of the poet's moods. His acceptance of coming death; his doubt and his angry moments; his lack of courage, and a regret not that he will die but that, in the present, he cannot bring much life, due to his illness, to his wife and cats...Musing as he waits; which is all that is left him: waiting for the end, in the light and in the darkness.

BONE PALACE BALLET, 1997

The title of this collection chosen by John Martin.

The book dives head-first into Buk's 1930's and 40's years of childhood and adolescence. The neighborhood streets: South 28th Street, Longwood Avenue, and Buk with friends and acquaintances as well as enemies: Baldy, Frank, Bill, Burns, Sanford, and Max. Plus Norman, Jimmy, and Max, who were all killed in the war.

From L. A. to those cities Buk visited while on the road (but not as hitch hiker like Kerouac—don't know as Buk EVER hitch hiked), and those small rented musty rooms he lived in and later spoke fondly of. "If I could close the door of that small room and be alone in it," he wrote, "I would begin to fill with something good: the unmolested tune of the singular self" (pg. 61 Miles). Back to that Philly bar again, opening-up the joint at 5 a.m., with the bartender, and closing-up at 2 a.m. Back to Texas with Barbara, Buk wife #1, and the scene there…

The poems slump a bit after initial sections. Flounder, it seems to me, in their own disgust. The poet's disgust: of life and other people—those untermenschen, little, bland, and boring—including most other poets. A disgust I am in sympathy with, but the harping leads into the Slough of Despond, and who, I ask, wants to stay, long, in the Slough of Despond?

A minor slump: soon, Bukowski is hitting the ball again to all fields. Line-drives, doubles, triples, and off the wall. Poems about what his fame hath wrought: letters, visitors, interviewers; praise and damnation. Meeting someone who is excited to see him. The poet maintains a certain sangfroid—which allows him to write of Hollywood and the celebrity-culture, unabashed by the famous and able to take accurate measure of the piranhas, narcissists, and others in the 'fame-game.' Not becoming subsumed by the whole scene or over-inflated by his own ego through an exalted sense of himself. Keeping his feet on the earth always.

This collection is to savor, especially the last 200 pages or so. I am awed, while reading, how seamlessly the words are laid down on the page, and the excellence of so many poems. While reading, I almost begin to inhabit the poet's space: his room, house, cats, wife (ha ha); like I've been invited in, asked to sit, given a glass of German wine (though I no longer drink) and told to relax and enjoy the show— the Bukowski home-movie.

THE CAPTAIN IS OUT TO LUNCH AND THE SAILORS HAVE TAKEN OVER THE SHIP, 1998.

A daily or nightly journal Buk kept in his 71st and 72nd years: 8-'91 to 2-93. The old barfly writing of reading Hume, Descartes, Sartre, and Kiekegaard…Smoking beedies and also going to the racetrack almost daily. The track, writing; his nine cats; his wife, and time spent writing poems and a novel—no more short stories. Re-airing of pet peeves, such as his dislike of most other poets—those vain, self-aggrandizing little worms…Writing of writers: Sherwood Anderson of the delightful line; Hemingway the humorless; Theodore Dreiser, the worst writer— on par with Faulkner and Thomas Wolfe (Dreiser wrote club-footed rickety prose, true, but who else, I ask you, in the annals of literature, had a bigger and greater heart than Dreiser?)

In an interesting aside Hank is contacted by a TV producer who wants to do a series using Hank's life as template. Hank considers the deal then backs out. Imagine William Bendix in the role. Or Ernest Borgnine!

No entries 8-3 to 9-15-'92 because Buk bit by a spider. At the emergency room he is given antibiotics. A treatment that reminds him of his treatment for TB and brings on painful memories, recorded in the journal.

Buk is at his most relaxed in this journal-writing. Writing still from the gut and with the occasional sparkle and roar. He had ability to make the mundane interesting—to make readers care about the world that he, and we, inhabit.

WHAT MATTERS MOST IS HOW WELL YOU WALK THROUGH THE FIRE, 1999.

The third of Bukowski's Black Sparrow posthumous publications. Poems of some less stellar moments in the poet's life—such as the time Jane peed her pants and passed out in the apartment building's elevator. Incidents that give a certain dreary tone to the work—not to say the poems are "bad." If written by anyone else they would be "good," but are mediocre Bukowski-poems (which is bad after one has read, as I have, so many excellent poems by Buk).

A poem mentions Picasso, another references Van Gogh, who is subject of a number of Buk-poems (Buk mistakenly believed Van Gogh used a shotgun to shoot himself—it was a pistol). A poem mentions a picture painted by "Eric Heckel," hung on Buk's wall. Eric Heckel is actually "Ernst Haeckel," a German expressionist-painter, S. D. Calonne points out (pg. 98 Calonne CHARLES BUKOWSKI), and the picture one Buk inherited from his parents.

As a draughtsman and painter himself, Buk evinces, in his work and life, little enthusiasm or interest in the visual arts. In one of his letters he mentions Klee, in another Mondrian; in a third he asks his correspondent who Munch is. One reference in correspondence to Miro (in connection to Hemingway), one to Cezanne, ditto Matisse, Manet, Renoir, Gauguin, and Pissaro. Multiple references to James Thurber whom Buk reservedly admired. Buk had an odd, to me, identification with Thurber who was of upper-middle-class provenance and part of the NEW YORKER magazine set. Buk's drawing are very much in the Thurber line, though Buk's much looser in execution than the controlled and smoothly non-fractal presentations of Thurber. Buk also admired the work of American-born cartoonist R. Crumb, who has illustrated a number of Bukowski works. (Crumb presenting Buk as somewhat chunky, like an ex-athlete gone to pot.) Buk wrote of Crumb's people as having a "wonderful juice and glow" (pg. 146 BUKOWSKI ON WRITING, Ed. Abel Debritto)

Toulouse Lautrec gets a poem: Lautrec may be the artist closest to Buk in subject matter usage: dance hall girls, courtesans, and characters of the demimonde. Also, like Buk, with his acne vulgaris, Lautrec had the disability of his shortened legs to contend with.

While living with his 1st wife Bukowski enrolled in a commercial art class. The class professor, Buk reports (pg. 46 BUKOWSKI ON WRITING, ed. Abel Debritto) stole one of Buk's drawing ideas and sold it commercially. Buk played with abstraction, and was a collagist of some ability—many of his letters assume collage form. The theme of his line drawings is the life and times of a caricatured male figure usually surrounded by Buk staples of bottle, cigar, cats, etc., and signifying and suggesting a great deal through use of the simple line. (BUKOWSKI ON WRITING, ed. A. Debritto, contains some superb Bukowski artwork).

Poems featuring life at Carlton Way neighborhood are plentiful. Carlton Way the low-rent district where Buk felt some comfort and also identification with, evident in his use of the pronoun "we" in reference to the place and its inhabitants—including a giant, 300-pound neighbor, a mentally-challenged acquaintance, and variety of ladies…

Attention to death, its ubiquity, has a large presence in the volume. Death not only as an end but as a constant companion too, a notion passed down from certain gloomy and romantic artists of the Fin de Siecle in Europe, a tradition that Buk, it could be said (and is, by S. D. Calonne, CHARLES BUKOWSKI) came out of, possibly inheriting, at least the notions—from his Germanic heritage—concepts from the variety of artistic movements under the umbrella term "Fin de Siecle."

OPEN ALL NIGHT, New Poems, 2000.

Poems about Buk and Linda Lee in Germany—the first, in the poetry, I've read of the trip (which Linda Lee liked, while Buk, the unhappy tourist, disliked, longing for home). The San Pedro scene: Buk's nights at the typer, writing; and if the writing is not coming then there is Plan B which is drinking heavily. The return of characters from Carlton Way: Big Sam, and Larry the Subnormal; racetrack –poems, of course; and freeway-poems…Some fine and funny poems, among them 'swivel chair.'

Much of the material, in this volume and others, has to do with the challenge of living, as a sensitive person, in a desensitized world. Dealing with the pain and frustration of existing in an often cold and inhospitable landscape of human beings. How to walk through the fire without being incinerated? How not to let the day by day triviality of existence extinguish the light of the soul? How to avoid jails, institutions, and an earlier death than necessary?

A series of poems about the old Beat poet Jack Micheline, whom Bukowski had some disparaging thoughts of. Bukowski generally distanced himself from the Beats, disliking their "groupism." He did make favorable comments about Corso and Ginsberg, once referring to the former as "a fine soul" and treating the latter with some deference, once calling him a "major talent"; and writing, in an essay published in Ole in 1960, of Ginsberg as the "most awakening force in American poetry since Whitman' (pg. 39 PORTIONS).

Buk mostly ignored Burroughs, who reportedly snubbed Buk. Though Buk said that Kerouac could not write well, and implied Kerouac's fame to be the result of his good looks ("like a rodeo cowboy") he paid a back-handed compliment to the Beat Daddy by not speaking of his writing. Buk disliked the overtly politicized act of Ginsberg's, and thought, on the whole, the Beats more concerned with taking a fame-shot than they were serious about writing (although Buk not adverse to fame-shot deals himself when opportunity arose). He also disliked what he saw as grandstanding by certain Beats—their vanity and "public posturing. Hucksters of the despoiled word" ('the Beats'). Micheline comes in for the heaviest of Buk's drubbings, being parodied in several

Buk poems for his brashness. In his poem 'the Poet' Buk criticizes Micheline for his habit of wearing a scarf—a kind of sartorial proclamation announcing exclusiveness, as in other Beats announcing themselves as "Poet"—as if it were a special category of human being, new genre type, somehow different, and superior to, all the non-poets—plumbers, postmen, podiatrists, those not wearing a beret or scarf or goatee or pigtail. What spoils the poet is "special treatment or his own idea that he is special," Bukowski wrote in his essay "Notes on the Life of an Aged Poet" (pgs. 121-28, PORTIONS). Of course, Bukowski considered himself to be a special case too and that is why he so often, in his relationships, acted the spoiled brat.

THE NIGHT TORN MAD WITH FOOTSTEPS, 2001.

This collection of poetry takes a while before it starts to cook: the first 250 pages are not bad, just not nearly as good as the final 100. Buk hits his stride in San Pedro poems. Linda, the 'wife,' or, "my woman" comes off as wise and funny—her barbs regularly deflating Buk's pomposity. The personalized poems are more entertaining than the generalized: 'the bore' and 'justice,' about the trips to Germany and France, are detailed and specific in the telling, full of succinct dialog, and contain a greater liveliness than earlier poems.

In the poem 'girl on the escalator' Buk adopts a Buddhist evaluation strategy regarding the young lovely, in skin-tight pants and blouse; viewing her elemental make-up not just the beauty, as in contemplating her intestines and other parts—some of the 32 bodily elements Buddhist monks, in lust, are advised to focus on to put out the fire of the defilement.

SIFTING THROUGH THE MADNESS FOR THE WORD, THE LINE, THE WAY, 2003.

Childhood memories of playing the Victrola in his parent's living room; watching the woman on the next door stoop. The brutal father and his assistant, the cold mother. Linda King enters screeching in 'this dog'; Linda's fat sister and Hank go at it, verbally. Hank back in the Post Office and at other old and pointless jobs. America at work, where they "rip out intestines, brain, and spirit" ('commence'), suck you dry, toss you aside…It is called the Capitalist system. Buk is the anti-American, a wrench in the guts of the machine. Enjoying the fruits of the system but disdaining the work ethic—the one preached to him by his old man; he sees through the profit motive to where it is really at, meaning knowing where the money goes and aware of the exclusion, at the trough, of the many in favor of the few. Bukowski gives his readers the view of a bottom-feeder in the chain, living off the scraps that trickle-down. He recorded the nightmare contained within the Dream.

In poems toward the end of the volume Buk begins to question his narcissistic self-involvement: the "hell," he writes, of himself. Weary from staring too long at his unfinished novel perhaps. Feeling "displaced" while at the racetrack, wondering why he is there—wondering why he is anywhere. Tired of his "contest with myself" ('escape'). His study and writing room become a room "full of ghosts" ('burning, burning'), he writes.

An existential crises and the thoughts of an older man, 70-71, with serious health issues, and knowing his time is nearly up. Doing hard labor "in solitary" ('like a dolphin'), "locked down…sit(ting) in my own shadow now."

THE FLASH OF LIGHTNING BEHIND THE MOUNTAIN, 2004.

Buk has become one of the "great drunks of the centuries" he writes ('tonight'). Talk about your grandiose Ubermensch! There are countless drunks: What makes Bukowski one of the greatest? The amount drunk or the fact he is still alive at 71 years old? Despite the amount.

Sitting in his San Pedro study, he takes another gulp of wine. Now, he is "full of wine," he writes; and full of himself too (I write).

These the poems of a "newly mellow recluse" sometimes "snarling in the dark."

His existential philosophy is laid out in the verse: there are no innocents, he claims, and hate is the only reality; there is no chance in life for anyone—none. It is a fixed game and life itself, big 'L,' is a zero, not to be accepted nor fought against, but only pondered. No god, capital 'G,' exists. Though the gods may. The "gods" who, Bukowski claims, have been good to him. Unclear the provenance of these gods; he says they are impish, and that "we are their toys" ('my big night on the town'). The gods have brought him luck, he comments; he might not be the happiest guy around but he IS the luckiest, he claims. His success the luck of the draw…Maybe he is right, and Einstein wrong: God does play dice with the Universe.

SOUCHING TOWARD NIRVANA, 2005.

Though Nirvana not a place but the extinction of craving—and good luck with that—it adds to a fitting title for the eschatological mutterings and murmurs of Buk in his 70th year. 'Slouching' is the operative word as Buk, given an 8-count after his TB trial, rises from the canvas to continue the good fight, though there is no hope of winning as the outcome is a forgone conclusion. 'Adios' is the final word of the book.

These poems are slighter than the works of previous posthumous volumes. Less body to them, more skeleton showing. Thinner versions of the same old stories, with variations on the themes (racetrack, freeway, childhood, young manhood, writing, etc.). The slightness is or should probably be expected in a 7th posthumously published volume.

COME ON IN, 2006.

This is the first of the posthumous poetry collections to acknowledge that John Martin edited the work.

Two of Bukowski's strengths as writer were clarity and accessibility. Some of the language in this volume is neither, because muddled, misplaced, and clumsy—atypical of Bukowski's writing. I offer a handful of examples: "keep it loose/with a great number of poems, try with all your heart"—try with all your heart! Buk rarely used 'heart' or 'soul' knowing how ambiguous those terms are; in the poem 'my song' he writes (or did he?) "fighting/with all your/heart and soul." A good Hallmark Card line. "one can't believe that/especially if one has felt as I have"—one can't? Why can't one? This is a poor joke: Martin has done an unconscionable editing/hatchet job. "You're floating out there in the white air"—since when? This from Buk? "those writers of poems/ that sound like poems/think that they there must/go around"—talk about awkwardness! "not to mention/vanity/or the need for/instantaneous/ approbation"—stogy academic language. Not my Bukowski. "we were out on the town/and we/went to this nice/house, lovely couple, etc./ anyhow, there were 7 or"—hear the redundancy? Cut 'we,' cut 'anyhow' and get to the point—smooth the flow, man. "they say they will do anything/and everything/for and to me/for as long as"—wow. 'for and to me for?' "I should be able to ignore…the dark shit/ (that despite the dark shit) floods my/brain"—say what?

Most of these examples taken from the first 50 or so pages. Examples of bad—lazy, ungrammatical, solecistic—language usage.

Making Buk sound like Rod McKuen is an insult to Buk; making Buk sound like a bad writer is a crime.

The book ends with Buk facing a return to the hospital after his cancer has returned. Poems that could be expected pour out: sad and dark.

A final coda urges acceptance of life as life is—the gamble of the days and the end: take it.

THE CONTINUAL CONDITION, 2009.

The 9th and last of the Bukowski estate's published collections.

A thin, 127 page volume, stuffed with repeats, poems previously published in other collections. An acknowledgement claims several of the poems previously published in broadsides.

A fair number of San Pedro-poems, some concerning Linda Lee, which is good as her appearance always adds something of interest. Other poems of the late-night duo of Bukowski and his typewriter (computer). Reflection on the act of writing: specifics of the moment: state of the room at, say, 1:34 a.m. A cat scratching, a far off dog's howl, the lights of boats in the harbor, cars on the freeway…A glass on the desk needing a refill of wine; a cigar in the ashtray and half-smoked; the radio playing a piece by some composer whom Buk usually knows. The Bee, or Bach, or Mozart, or—best of all, for Buk—Mahler. The usual set-up, in other words. But always with a twist, a variation on whatever theme—thereby saving Buk's work from being boring.

Buk in his final year: writing while at the lip of the grave. "Staring," he writes, "into the eye of an empty bottle" ('bayonets in candlelight').

STORM FOR THE LIVING AND THE DEAD, 2017.

These poems were resurrected by Abel Debritto, some from as far back as 1959. A number of which should have been allowed to lie where found. A handful of excellent ones, however, among the detritus: 'tongue cut,' 'I live to write and now I'm dying,' 'the glory days,' 'song for this softly sweeping sorrow,' and 'my America, 1936.'

'I thought I was going to get some' the most frankly homo-erotic poem of Buk's career (more so even than the poem in which Hank sodomizes Baldy).

A Carson McCullers-poem: "dead/of/drink and/greatness/the heart/ like a boomerang" ('T.H.I.A.L.H.'). McCullers the only female writer Buk ever praised in print. He mentions H.D., Diane Wakoski, Kay Boyle, but praises only McCullers. He did conduct a correspondence with a number of women in the arts: Ann Menebroker, Sheri Martinelli, Kay Johnson, Joan Jobe Smith, and Linda King, among others. Something about the sad atmosphere and feeling of loss in McCuller's work found favor with Buk who has his own saga of sadness—but much of riotous joy too. Many—most—of McCuller's characters are odd-balls, outsiders; mutes, dwarfs, giants, hunchbacks, criminals, androgynous sibyls; physically-challenged and psychically existing in netherworlds estranged from the quotidian: like Buk as a young man in his rooming house rooms, living with the shades pulled down, self-isolated from a world he found threatening, confusing, and not worth his effort to accommodate.

In another poem Buk speaks of McCuller's "books about/the cruelty/of loveless love," something Buk applied to himself when speaking of his childhood as well as nearly all his shack-jobs of the 70's and 80's.

CONCLUSION

Few are the modern writers able to lay down the hard clean line with the immediacy and visceral power of Bukowski. Hunter S. Thompson was one (though Thompson's over-identification as a child of the 1960's limited the scope of interest in his productions). Raymond Carver often brought a Bukowski-like immediacy to his poems and stories, though the voice less raw, more detached emotionally thus at a further remove than Bukowski's tone. Fred Exley brought as great an amount of riotous living into his work as well as a personality as outsized as Bukowski's but as stylists they were quite different—Exley more of a classical writer: a maximalist rather than, like Buk, a minimalist.

One might begin reading Bukowski with the thought or idea of Buk as a primitive, but sooner or later one realizes that all of Buk's critical stances are fully thought-out. Through the rough edges and vulgarity shines forth a percipient intelligence that belies all notions of Buk as untutored barbarian. His knowledge of literature, and of life, was formidable and most of his critical stances I find spot-on. He was both book-smart and street wise; writing this study I have come to realization and appreciation of the depth of his thought.

As autodidact and, I guess you could say, a "natural" talent, he learned his trade from reading other writers: his "masters," such as Celine, Jeffers, Dos, Lawrence, Hamsun, Fante, and the early Saroyan and Hemingway. From them he acquired ideas of form and examples of attitude that he incorporated into his own work.

Few modern-age poets could be considered peers of Bukowski: a better comparison by analogy, could be made, I think, between Bukowski and the German philosopher Nietzsche. Nietzsche conducted a scorched-earth policy toward all other philosophers; Bukowski likewise toward all contemporaneous poets. Each felt themselves the end-all and be-all of their respective fields. Bukowski condemned centuries of literature out of hand as farce and scam, and the "tradition" of letters, as passed-down, a dirty trick played on those who came later. The ubiquitously avowed greatest of all figure in English-speaking literature, Shakespeare, was dismissed by Bukowski as being of little relevance or even interest. And those in the tradition whom he admired, like Aiken, Auden, Spender, et al. he praised but not without reservation. Nietzsche's cataclysmic comedy of "tragic laughter" was adopted whole-heartedly by Bukowski. To him the humorless (like late-Hem) were anathema. As were the portentous (late-Hem, again).

The Ubermensch is, ultimately, a monster: a great spider spinning fearsomely from some centralized web. Castigating and reviling all the untermenschen. A monstrous egomania leaves the Ubermensch no choice but a wholesale disparagement. He exists on the sufferance of others, but only if the talent he brings to the table is sufficiently awesome—enough to arouse, delight, entertain, or teach. Buk succeeded in all 4 areas. He also not only humanized modern poetry but democratized it as well. His work brought people into the arena who had no previous interest in poetry and no conception that it could speak to their condition—as Buk's work does to so many. Through the clarity of his language and frankness of his voice he made poetry accessible and thus relevant to many who felt excluded by the in-speak of poetic diction, and phraseology, and obscurantism. Though beginning, in his work, using language self-consciously "poetic," he evolved over the years until, by the end years, his verse had become Zen-like in omniscience. His language cut so finely and so close to the bone as to make meaning unmistakable.

Bukowski imitators among poets are legion. But, as Buk knew, and Charlie Parker reputedly once said: "you got to live it to play it." The living of his life fed Bukowski's work—the two inextricably mixed. He was never encased in an ivory tower looking down at the masses, exempt from so-called 'normal' life—the working life of so-called "everyday people" living, dying, surviving best they can in the meat-market of capitalist America. Buk knew them well, and though disliking the 'people' in to-to, was empathetic to the common plight of working people and others struggling in the system. Though claiming to be apolitical his sympathies were clearly with the underdogs.

Though Buk had a less than sterling character (whose IS "sterling"?) he was able, in his writings anyway, to come across as loving father, caring husband, and generous friend. He never threw stones at anyone—knowing the fragility of his own house. He called himself a "coward" and wrote unapologetically of his own weaknesses—his character flaws, if you like. In letters to Canadian poet Al Purdy Buk dismissed notions of guilt and remorse—necessary exclusions if one is to remain an active alcoholic (which is to say "successful alcoholic"). Like most alkies, Bukowski was sly and savvy, and able to keep a job long-term and a roof over his head. This despite numerous run in's with the law and several alcohol related driving violations. He also, though dumb luck or slyness, kept himself out of jail for length-y amounts of time (although there was an 18 day stay in county jail in Philadelphia).

His relationships with women were mostly abysmal, though he maintained a long-term engagement and marriage with his 2nd wife Linda Lee, which, by his own account and hers, a happy coupling, though not without occasional storminess. A misogynistic streak in his character—a believer in the old double-standard which consigned male and female specific roles, developed, as I previously argued, from an unsatisfactory relationship with an emotionally distant mother. Jane, an attractive though dissolute and so-called "crazy" woman, held a drink in hand when first she and Hank met. An attractive woman holding a drink was Hank's ideal in femininity. A good relationship for Hank until Jane lost her good looks and then died through abuse of alcohol. Barbara Frye, Buk's first wife—married in a shot-gun ceremony—seemed particularly unsuited for Bukowski, and vice-versa (she not alcoholic). He moved on to other, more troubled, females, including the cyclonic

Linda King, a drama-queen nonpareil (Buk was King). These ships in the night—Buk afloat too—collided and sunk with regularity. Pam O'Brien, aka 'Cupcakes' came out of a girly magazine and Bukowski's adolescent fantasies; unfortunately, for both, Buk was in his 50's at the time…Human relationships are hard. Ask any human.

John Webb once said that reading Bukowski's work spoiled him, John, for other poets. I feel similarly. My patience for verse intentionally obscure and making use of verbiage to say little or nothing is slight. I do not, as I once did, feel obligated to plow ahead reading the incomprehensible scribblings of poets, celebrated or not. I turn quickly away from language games certain tricky au courant poets seem to enjoy playing. I no longer always consider it my inadequacy when I fail to comprehend a poem (it may be the poet's, no?). Snobbery in poetry circles must be fought against as well as in the public sphere. Pretense in writing is an un-reprievable act, and one the critic is obligated to crush. Buk fought against both with hammer blows of his typewriter.

Thank the 17 gods Bukowski prayed to that we have his work and example to carry us into the future.

SELECTED BIBLIOGRAPHY

Works by Charles Bukowski:

THE LAST NIGHT OF THE EARTH POEMS

DANGLING IN THE TOURNAFORTIA

WAR ALL THE TIME, Poems 1981-1984

FACTOTUM

SOUTH OF NO NORTH

HAM ON RYE

NOTES OF A DIRTY OLD MAN

THE ROOMINGHOUSE MADRIGALS

*PULP

PLAY THE PIANO LIKE A PERCUSSION INSTRUMENT
UNTIL THE FINGERS BEGIN TO BLEED A BIT

LOVE IS A DOG FROM HELL

BURNING IN WATER DROWNING IN FLAME

YOU GET SO ALONE AT TIME THAT IT JUST MAKES
SENSE

HOT WATER MUSIC

HOLLYWOOD

BRING ME YOUR LOVE (Illustrated by R. Crumb)

*THE CONTINUAL CONDITION

WOMEN

POST OFFICE

MOCKINGBIRD WISH ME LUCK

*BETTING ON THE MUSE

THE DAYS RUN AWAY LIKE WILD HORSES OVER THE HILLS

*THE CAPTAIN IS OUT TO LUNCH AND THE SAILORS HAVE TAKEN OVER THE SHIP

*WHAT MATTERS MOST IS HOW WELL YOU WALK THROUGH THE FIRE

*OPEN ALL NIGHT

*NIGHT TORN MAD WITH FOOTSTEPS

*SIFTING THROUGH THE MADNESS FOR THE WORD, THE LINE, THE WAY

*THE FLASH OF LIGHTNING BEHIND THE MOUNTAIN

*SLOUCHING TOWARD NIRVANA

*THE PEOPLE LOOK LIKE FLOWERS AT LAST

*COME ON IN

(*) Denotes posthumous publication

CRITICAL WORKS

CHARLES BUKOWSKI, Barry Miles, 2005, Virgin Books, Ltd, London

CHARLES BUKOWSKI, Locked in the Arms of a Crazy Life, Howard Sounes, 1998, Grove Press, New York.

CHARLES BUKOWSKI, Gay Brewer, Twayne's United States Author's Series, 1997, Twayne Publishers, Simon & Schuster Macmillan, New York.

BUKOWSKI, A Life, Neeli Cherkovski, 2020, Black Sparrow Press, Boston.

ART,SURVIVAL, AND SO FORTH, The Poetry of Charles Bukowski, Jules Smith, 2000, Wrecking Ball Press, UK.

CHARLES BUKOWSKI, Critical Lives, David Stephen Catonne, 2012, Reaktion Books, London.

COLLECTIONS OF BUKOWSKI WORK

CHARLES BUKOWSKI, Absence of the Hero, Uncollected Stories & Essays, Vol. II, Ed. By David Stephen Calonne, 2010, City Lights Books.

CHARLES BUKOWSKI, Portions From A Wine-Stained Notebook, Uncollected Stories and Essays, 1944-1990, Ed. By David Stephen Calonne, 2008, City Lights Books, San Francisco.

MORE NOTES OF A DIRTY OLD MAN, The Uncollected Columns, Charles Bukowski, edited by David Stephen Calonne, 2011, City Lights Books.

THE MATHEMATICS OF THE BREATH AND THE WAY: On Writers and Writing. Charles Bukowski. Edited by David Stephen Calonne, 2018, City Lights Books.

STORMS FOR THE LIVING AND THE DEAD, Uncollected and Unpublished Poems Charles Bukowski, edited by Abel Debritto, 2017, Harper Collins Publishers, N.Y., New York.

CHARLES BUKOWSKI ON WRITING, edited by Abel Debritto, 2015, HarperCollins Publishers, N.Y., New York.

CHARLES BUKOWSKI ON DRINKING, edited by Abel Debritto, 2019, HarperCollins Publishers, N.Y., New York.

ESSENTIAL BUKOWSKI, Poetry, Selected and Edited by Abel Debritto, 2016, HarperCollins Publishers, N.Y., New York.

BUKOWSKI'S LETTERS

SCREAMS FROM THE BALCONY. Selected Letters 1960-1970, edited by Seamus Cooney, 1993, Black Sparrow Press, Santa Rosa, CA.

LIVING ON LUCK, Selected Letters 1960-1970, vol. II, edited by Seamus Cooney, 2000, Black Sparrow Press, Santa Rosa, CA.

REACH FOR THE SUN, Selected Letters 1978-1994, vol. III, edited by Seamus Cooney, 1999, Black Sparrow Press, Santa Rosa, CA.

BUKOWSKI, Selected Letters Vol. IV, 1987-1994, edited by Seamus Cooney, 2005, Virgin Books, London.

ADDITIONAL SOURCES

A DARING YOUNG MAN: A Biography of William Saroyan, John Leggett, 2002, Alfred A. Knopf, N.Y., New York.

FULL OF LIFE, A Biography of John Fante, Stephen Cooper, 2000, North Point Press, Farrar, Straus, and Giroux, N.Y., New York.

THE MAN WHO WASN'T THERE, A Life of Ernest Hemingway, Tauris Parke, 2018, Bloomsbury Publishing, London.

HENRY MILLER, Spirit & Flesh, Wayne F. Burke, 2022, Cyberwit.Net, India.

9 788119 228089